ACE IV

Arresting,
Contemporary
stories by
Emerging writers

edited by
Julia Prendergast,
Eileen Herbert-Goodall
& Deb Wain

RECENT
WORK
PRESS

ACE Anthology IV: Arresting, Contemporary stories by Emerging writers
Recent Work Press
Canberra, Australia

Copyright © the authors, 2023

ISBN: 9780645973204 (paperback)

A catalogue record for this
book is available from the
National Library of Australia

Cover design: Thomas Hamlyn-Harris
Set by: Thomas Hamlyn-Harris

recentworkpress.com

Australasian Association of Writing Programs

RECENT
WORK
PRESS

Contents

Introduction

Julia Prendergast (on behalf of the editorial team)

Gordon Weaver asks, 'In how small a space can [we] create the *felt presences* that animate successful stories?' (Shapard & Thomas, 1983, p. 228, emphasis added). The concept of felt presences is at the heart of the contributions in *ACE IV: Arresting, Contemporary Stories by Emerging Writers*.

Across the collection, the authors examine the conundrum and contradiction of human experience through carefully crafted detail. The brevity of short-form writing makes it an apt vessel for capturing the haunting incompleteness of human experience. Through flash and traditional length short stories—fiction and life writing, as well as hybrid forms of storytelling—there is a compelling ebb and tow of ideas, as focalised through highly idiosyncratic 'register[s] of intelligence' (Wharton, 1997, p. 63). The authors work deftly, paying due homage to the crucial relationship between idiosyncratic voice and sharply rendered detail—cultivating narrative features with intuitive hands and minds, fashioning abstracted realities that linger beyond the final lines of the text.

Editing is an act of deep listening—it's deeply privileged work. The contributions leave us reeling. We ask: How it is possible that story-work can enter our affect cycle as if it were lived experience? In these stories, we bear witness to the creative use of language as an act of homage to an otherwise irresolvable idea. It has been our great pleasure to listen to these authors, to have our empathic compass expanded by their art.

We acknowledge the generous support of the Australasian Association of Writing Programs (AAWP), the peak academic body representing the discipline of Creative Writing in Australasia. AAWP offers a suite of national and international prizes and publication pathways, in support of emerging and established writers and translators, in partnership with Ubud Writers and Readers Festival (UWRF), Australian Short Story Festival (ASSF), the University of Western Australia Press (UWAP), *WESTERLY* Magazine and *Voiceworks*/Express Media. Many of the contributions in this collection were submitted to AAWP prizes: *https://aawp. org.au/news/opportunities/*.

We are grateful to those who provided funds in support of this project. Thank you to the board of the Australian Short Story Festival (ASSF), who received the following grant funding: Restart Investment to Sustain and Expand (RISE). ASSF allocated a portion of grant funding in support of this collection, in keeping with the following grant imperatives: providing remunerated publication pathways and networking opportunities for emerging and under-represented writers from diverse cultural backgrounds and providing mentorship and income for two emerging editors. Thank you to the Executive Committee of the Australasian Association of Writing Programs (AAWP), who also contributed funds in support of this project. We deeply appreciate the combined commitment of AAWP and ASSF, working together in support of emerging writers and editors.

Thank you to Shane Strange, publisher at Recent Work Press, for publishing this collection. Thank you to Thomas Hamlyn-Harris for his expertise in cover design and layout. Finally, thank you to the hilarious and relentlessly delightful Eileen Herbert-Goodall and Deb Wain—for their generosity and meticulous attention to detail, for editorial sisterhood and fine company.

Wharton, E. (1997). *The writing of fiction*, Touchstone: Simon & Schuster.

Weaver, G. (1983). Gordon Weaver. In R. Shapard & J. Thomas (Eds.), *Sudden fiction: American short-short stories* (pp. 228–29). Gibbs Smith.

And Then the Tide Turns

Supatra Walker

The tide has turned. According to the tide chart, it turned just before noon, heading for its lowest point at ten past five this afternoon. All week I've watched the succession of tides. The sea recedes, then returns, in a rhythm too slow to be perceptible, as though beyond the harbour mouth it inhales and gathers for the next, slow exhale. I scan the exposed pebble-strewn mudflats of this shallow inlet, a burnished mirror of steel and black. The turning tides, measured and imperturbable, allay the pictures playing repeatedly in my mind, images and sounds of my father in the last hours of his life: the chesty rattle, the long silence and, finally, a gasp for breath. His eyes were closed. They'd taken his false teeth, the top ones. I'd never seen him without his teeth. In profile he was almost a stranger, his mutterings unintelligible. I held his right hand, gently rubbing his chest, his grip still firm. His left hand lay limp and useless by his side. He had lost awareness of his left side the afternoon they found him slumped beside his bed, four days from the time he shuffled into this nursing home, wide-eyed at the luxuriousness of the thick plush carpet and the chandelier in the foyer.

'Can we afford this?' he'd asked. We'd assured him. He thought it was a five-star hotel, although he knew he was there because my diminutive Thai mother could no longer care for him, as she had done for seven years when his aortic valve began to fail. The result was a series of small strokes followed by dementia. More recently he'd begun to hallucinate, a halo of confusion and paranoia enveloped him. To strangers, he appeared well, but the strokes robbed him of the abilities that defined him. He was an electrical engineer, a computer programmer, a boat builder: a man who could turn his considerable skill and intellect to almost any problem. Over the years we witnessed his frustration as he struggled to perform even the simplest of tasks. A small DIY bookshelf turned into a two-day fracas as he battled to follow the instructions and align the pieces.

'He don't know how to use the screwdriver,' Mum remarked. 'He can't make the screw go in. His hand go this way and that way, and all over the place. I finish it for him and he was so embarrassed.'

His life became dominated by a grinding regime of weekly trips to the local pathology practice where his warfarin levels were monitored, then to the GP who would adjust his medication accordingly. Lung and urinary tract infections would see him hospitalised from time to time and surgeons were still extracting skin cancers from his head and neck, a legacy of New Zealand's war in the Pacific Theatre. My parents' days were divided: those when he could leave the house and others when the diuretics confined him close to a toilet. My mother became a pill counter, carefully separating the various medications into correct dosages administered at very particular times of the day. We watched as the strain began to crush my mother, the small but stoic woman who had held our family together for over fifty years. Old age physically claimed my father. It sucked at his fat and skin, as well as his countenance and spirit, shrinking and diminishing him. Mum grumbled that he was difficult to engage in conversation and would shuffle restlessly from room to room, from window to window, in his pyjamas and dressing gown. He complained about lack of sleep, although he slept for a good deal of the day. He called his night attire his 'lurking clothes' because my mother would accuse him of doing so.

I flew in from Australia with my youngest daughter in early May, two days after he was admitted to hospital with a chest infection and kidney failure. My eldest daughter and niece would follow two days later. His cardiac specialist said he had end-stage aortic stenosis. It was just a matter of time. But somehow he pulled a miracle recovery, perhaps buoyed by all the attention, walking out of hospital on steady legs with a straight back. Ironically, because he was still mobile, it was thought he best be admitted to a care facility, rather than sent back home. However, few facilities can safely care for people like Dad: those who appear strong and lucid, until they do or say something odd. In Dad's case, his nightly rummaging in the drawers of the other residents raised some flags.

'The bloody Australians are stealing our warfarin,' he informed me. 'They come in at night and steal the urine of all those men.' He pointed towards the four other men in his shared hospital room. 'There is blood everywhere.'

Dad was discharged, courtesy of the government, to a luxury retirement village with a purpose-built, locked dementia unit and a hospital wing staffed by registered nurses, the first of its type in the Bay of Plenty, a sixty-kilometre round trip from home. The food was prepared by chefs. Dad had his own room and ensuite. We brought photographs in white frames, his favourite chair and some of his precious books. He flirted with the nurses and drank a beer at Happy Hour while warbling along at the Wednesday afternoon sing-song. For four short days, it seemed he had settled into his new home. On that fateful day, we'd dressed him in new trousers and he was pleased with himself, apparently having the time of his life. I began to entertain thoughts of returning to Australia. It was late afternoon when we were called back, two hours after we'd left him, to find him slumped in a chair in the lounge room, drooling and paralysed down his left side. His left arm lay motionless on his lap and the whole left side of his face had dropped.

'After that performance I should've just exited stage left, shouldn't I,' he slurred. He had trouble holding his head upright but his gaze was clear and lucid. Someone had tried to feed him soup and there were corn kernels in his mouth. Why in God's name? I couldn't quiet the questions rolling around in my mind.

I hear a shrill *kleep kleep kleep* coming from the estuary below. On the other side of this small inlet, about a kilometre to the northwest, a group of pied oystercatchers and stilts have taken up permanent residence on a sandy rock-strewn bar. Every now and again a few birds launch from their vantage point to fish on the eastern shore. They cry as they fly, their raucous calls echoing across the estuary. Through the field glasses, I watch them, their reflections on the polished silver water are perfect, so much so that I am sometimes unable to tell the difference between bird and mirror image. I search the reedy shorelines hoping to see godwits and dotterels, though I don't know if I'd recognise one if I did.

The house I am staying in is located on the south side of an inlet. My sister rents this old farmhouse and teaches at the small, two-teacher primary school of Kinohaku, just a three-minute drive around the inlet to the east. My brother-in-law, a builder, has worked around these parts for years. During the day I have the house to myself. Occasionally a car sweeps by on the road just below the house. But for the odd vehicle and the busy chittering of birds, my days here have been blissfully quiet. A pair of fantails flit in and out of the willow beside the driveway. A magpie warbles somewhere in the trees behind. This is the New Zealand of my youth. Fantails and magpies, bellbirds and kererū, the plump New Zealand pigeons.

At times, this small valley echoes with the song of birds I can't identify. I spend valuable hours searching web pages for birds I hope to see. I become distracted by the Pelagic birds that visit and inhabit this part of the west coast of the North Island. I have seen, through the glasses, the white-faced heron as well as the larger white heron, various types of shags, ducks, and gulls as well as oystercatchers and stilts. There are Canadian geese that have taken residence here in New Zealand in pest proportions. They can be seen sunning themselves on the grass-covered sheep paddocks close to freshwater dams and streams. They share these areas with the pukeko, the ubiquitous purple swamphen. Solitary falcons skim the exposed shoreline of flax and reeds. From the scrubby wattles below comes the unmistakable song of the tūī bird, a melodious bell-like gong interspersed with crackles, clicks, coughs and whistles.

When the tide is at its lowest, the estuary is a series of permanent channels surrounded by silvery mudflats. In this inlet, the sea recedes almost entirely, leaving one small main channel and a series of serpentine rivulets. A pair of spur-winged plovers wade quietly in one of these, bathing and showering the air with sprays that catch the sun and sparkle like diamonds. They seem more at ease than in the paddocks where they usually nest. Sometimes I hear their piercing alarm calls at night.

'Help, help,' my father called in a feeble voice. Finding strength, he rolled onto his left side, clawing at the wall. I slid a hand under his pyjama top and stroked the dehydrated skin of his back. He rolled back. Standing, I caught his arm and leaned over to stroke his face.

'It's okay, Dad, you're safe. We're all here.'

We had been taking turns by his bedside through the long, adrenaline-fuelled week following his stroke.

He opened his eyes, their once marble-blue sharpness now dim. Pulling his arm away, he slowly tapped my chest. He groaned, his face contorting. I took his hand and pressed it to the divot in my left chest, where the tissue is thinnest, where my heart can be felt beating in a gap between the ribs. I held his hand there for a long time. For a time he was quiet.

'You need to be careful, lass,' he said, 'they are ...' he searched for words, '... brand new,' he said finally. I knew what he was trying to say. He cried, as though he were somehow responsible.

'It doesn't really hurt anymore,' I said, referring to the double mastectomy I had in mid-February, a month after the first surgery, subsequent to another breast cancer diagnosis. This time it was a tumour in the left breast and six years after the first lump that was found in my right. The prospect of more radiation and painful mammograms, extending into an uncertain future, wearied me. I decided that removing both breasts would afford me some relief. I was sick of watching my back, of the ongoing vigilance and fear. I had kept quiet about the diagnosis and surgery, only telling my parents about my decision to have the double mastectomy during a

Skype session a few days before the surgery. They agreed it was a sane and considered decision. I didn't want breast reconstruction. The combination of numbness and sensitivity of the skin on my chest and under my shoulder blades makes any tight clothing uncomfortable. Pain and fatigue are features of my waking life. Because of that, I don't wear a bra or prosthesis. The scars that begin just under my armpits jag down to my breastbone where they are separated by an inch of skin. In the bathroom mirror, when I hold both arms above my head, the scars appear as two straight lines. With my arms by my sides, they remind me of the shags I see perched on the shopping trolleys on Throsby Creek, in Newcastle, when they hang their wings out to dry.

His eyes closed and I could see them moving under his papery, wafer-thin eyelids. His mouth was open. I placed his hand back on his chest and reached for the water glass, wiping his lips with a swab stick, urging him to swallow some water. He responded, sucking weakly. He stopped breathing and we waited.

I step out onto the front deck of the house and draw in a breath of cool air. It is oddly sweet and smoky from the wood fire burning in the lounge room. Far to the north, I see the unmistakable pointed peak of Mt Karioi. Two million years silent, the eruptions of Mt Karioi helped create much of the coastal flats in the region. Between us are the vast harbours of Kawhia and Aotea. Kawhia Harbour, of which this inlet is just a small part, is an area of over sixty square kilometres, and one of three harbours on the sparsely populated west coast of the North Island. At this time of year, the beginning of winter, the sun follows a low trajectory from northeast to northwest, its angle accentuating the steely greyness of water. For most of the week, the weather has been mild with lengthy periods of clear skies. Today a smear of high cloud against the azure-blue promises a picturesque sunset. This is the sort of view that is hard to ignore. I spend my days moving between the kitchen and lounge room, and then to the table on the front deck. I'm captivated by the scene that stretches out in front of me, an inlet bound by a range of scrubby hills and farmland, their reflection changing the colour of the water, sometimes a creamy jade, at other times blue-green. The silveriness is ever-present, especially on days like today when there is barely a breeze. Directly ahead, at the top of the inlet, the main harbour is obscured by a spit of land dense with vegetation: pittosporums, hebes, flaxes, tea trees, tree ferns and cabbage trees, and stands of the ancient kahikateas, the native non-resinous conifers thought to date back to the Jurassic age.

Talk to anyone around here and 'Jurassic' rolls off their tongues like 'café' does in my far-away home, Newcastle, Australia. I've been away for over a month. I have a large boil on my temple, my hair is in desperate need of a cut and I've turned into a moody, bad-tempered woman with a short fuse. I can't blame that entirely on the memories catching me unaware, threatening to cut me down at the knees, the tears that spring from nowhere and strand me in toilets. There are days dominated by waves of grief and conflicting emotions—relief, sadness, guilt and an overwhelming feeling of furious helplessness— moments when I wish I was somewhere else entirely.

'Do you like this place?' Dad asked my mother. 'I found this place for you,' he said with a shake of his forefinger.

'Oh, I luff it here,' she answered. She was holding his hand, her head resting on his right shoulder. He kissed her on the forehead.

'You tole me you find a beautiful place for me.' She said 'beautiful' in a high, sing-song voice.

They talked quietly and then I heard him exclaim, 'Oh the crabs! The big crabs. Your chilli crabs were the best in the world!' His eyes sparkled and he laughed with a strength that surprised me.

'You go find us a nice place with lots of fish and crabs, Al,' Mum instructed him.

'Somewhere like this?' he asked. 'Will you come with me?'

'I have tings to do, dear,' my mother answered. 'You find us a nice place by the sea and I join you later.'

'Oh yes, somewhere with big crabs! Snap, snap,' he said, making scissor motions with his good hand, a broad smile on his face.

My sister ducked her head and stared hard at her iPad, glitter in her eyes.

Snap, snap.

In the cove below the house, a family of kingfishers perches on a large tree branch stranded there in the last storm. From their vantage point, they venture to skim the mudflats. Their flights are short. They return to the branch with prey in their strong, black beaks: crabs, mud snails and other estuarine crustaceans.

In a few days I will drive back to Mt Maunganui, the once-sleepy coastal city that has been 'home' to our family for thirty-five years. The place that my father found for my mother, where he had wanted us all together again as a family. On Sunday he would have turned ninety. The party had been planned for months. We were all going to be there, much to his bemusement.

'They're planning a bloody big shindig,' he said wryly. 'I'm not sure I'm looking forward to that.'

Instead, we will have a quiet meal and then spread his ashes on the outgoing tide, from the jetty not far from the place where we first lived back in 1978. We imagine that he will be caught up in the tide as it withdraws through the mouth of Pilot Bay, past the bronze statue of Tangaroa, the god and protector of the sea, past the extinct volcano that is Mauao and finally into the warm currents to the South Pacific.

'Go and find that beautiful place, Alex,' my mother will say.

I watch the day closing and the setting sun turns the silvery-grey of the estuary to a soft gold. Above, the clouds are on fire and the sky is an intense blue. In the distance, the shrill cries of birds can be heard as they return to their sanctuary on the rocky bar. I imagine that through the narrow channel of the harbour mouth and out beyond the thundering breakers, the sea has fully inhaled.

In Search of Murakami

Alicia Sometimes

If you can write, you're not fixed. You can be anybody else—you have that possibility.

Haruki Murakami

Moments, splintered in microscale.

I arrived in Tokyo this morning, wanting to immerse myself in this labyrinthine city—write a story about Haruki Murakami—only now, I have nine hours left before flying back home. My friend Anna is sick, a sudden and unbearable diagnosis, but nothing I can do effectively from here. I need to get home to her but can't just yet, so the afternoon streets of Tokyo will have to distract me. My eyes, swollen and raw, register the way to the trains.

Anna and I are equally exhilarated exploring new places. Everything expands when travelling. Not just the linings of swollen bags or the pages of scrawled notebooks but the weight of every personal exchange. All components of the universe seem to be in flux: a point of view once held fiercely falls to your feet on a dirt road, strangers become a kindred tribe and your mind unfolds the past into one open thought.

For solace, I attempt to map Murakami's mind and write something for Anna.

Clasping a copy of *Norwegian Wood,* I look up at all the train station signs as if they are markings of my literary treasure hunt.

Looping my way to the Yamanote line, I follow the lime green signs closely. As I quicken to the end, I see two people embracing and weeping. I stop for a moment to write. A cartographer needs to assess the terrain in front of them.

'Can we walk by the river one last time?' The stranger looks down at her watch.

'Yes,' he says, reaching into his pocket for a mint, 'I think we should.'

Mapping the moments of fragility and loss in Murakami's books, I try to sew one broken love affair onto another. Writing one baseball allusion next to one jazz note, I place a verb of isolation next to a noun dripping in muscular mantra. I select random words from his books: *contrasts, memories, battle* and make lists. My words are forming shapes but not whole suppositions. Murakami with his pellucid prose, me with muddied metaphors.

Anna is weaving into the threads of my narrative: our last conversation about her career, her favourite songs, our meeting place in the city. Someone knocks into me as they beeline for the end of the coffee queue. My notebook falls in front of a vending machine. The sign reads: クラナド, advertising canned bread. The poses of the characters on the cans and flavours draw me in: butter, chocolate, banana and strawberry.

A woman carrying too many shopping bags stops abruptly. 'Take me away,' she says.

'Excuse me? *Sumimasen ...*'

'Take this away!' The lady points to my notebook. 'It's in my way.' I apologise and move further away from the machine. I imagine myself as quick and bright as a pulsar's whirling tendrils, but I must appear clumsy and deliberate, an emotional shopper at the gate of infinite possibilities.

The woman pays for the bread and blends in with the straggling commuters. I hear Liszt's Petrarch's Sonnet 47 from *Years of Pilgrimage* coming out of the platform speakers. I want to stop everything and dance but think better of it.

Tokyo is familiar to me. I lived here for six months with a local family. I was nine. Everything I remember is from the camera lens of a child: Doraemon with his time travel stories, Arale-Chan and her super-sonic strength and the *randoseru,* the red school backpacks. Every Saturday after school finished and we had scrubbed the floors, I returned home to sugary cereal. It was waiting for me the instant I walked through the door. Travel has turned these time capsules into single pictures—photographs of emotion pegged upon a fine string.

I must appear prosaic and unremarkable to passers-by with my edition of this well-worn book, my pen and the same demeanour of thousands of tourists before me. This look wears the clothes of a holiday, but I swear my intention was meant to be more long-lasting.

Walking out of the station, the chaos morphs into human calligraphy. The Shibuya Crossing is wild and enigmatic but still has structure. Standing here, I remember all the movies featuring this scene with flickering neon and bodies shimmering at light speed.

'*Sore wa wakarimasu ka?*' someone asks me. I do understand but language comes to me in tiny torn-up pieces. Sentences flip and turn themselves around. Everyone smiles, especially at my awkward phrasing.

'Yes, I think I know,' I say. But do I comprehend Murakami? Is that what the voice meant?

I keep steady ground, reminding myself to breathe. Anna would appreciate this trek. What did Murakami say kept him healthy? 'Music and cats,' I say out loud, 'music and cats.'

A man sporting an oversized dinosaur hoodie grins and asks if I need help.

'Come with me,' he adds.

He takes me by the hand that is holding Murakami. He notices the title and says he has an exact copy.

We drink green tea in a warm *kissaten* close by. He talks about jogging and allegorical misunderstandings. He whispers, 'Will you remember that I existed, and that I stood next to you here like this?'

I imagine spending the rest of my life with this stranger. As I slide my hand around the rim of the teacup in a clockwise motion, I tell him about getting home to Anna. I realise these feelings about fate are as fleeting as our crumbling cake. We both know our stories will diverge.

As we pay, he says, 'You must come back to Japan.' I know I will, but not back to him. I say goodbye as he pulls his hood over his ears and waves back slowly with his pinkie.

'Hope your friend is okay,' he says. His kindness tucks into the sides of my ribcage.

Murakami's mind is taking too long to map and I must move faster. I need to go to the airport soon but I want to return to Anna with something of note, a story to uplift.

I'm not sure where to go next, so I randomly choose a letter of the alphabet. H. Yes, the first place with the letter H is where I will visit.

The smell of ramen is punctuating my steps back to the station. Every pitch of conversation is a drumbeat, each laugh becomes a refrain and the loudspeakers form swelling crescendos. I want to write more about the crowd's music but it's too difficult among the bustle. I spot the sign with the name of my new destination.

I narrowly make the next train and sit down beside a young girl with a large umbrella. She looks at the floor the minute I get out my pen. I write that I am a pendulum moving back and forth, slicing through time. No past, no future, only now, never pushing further than where I began.

These sentences are not getting to the heart of my sadness and I'm on the verge of interweaving metaphors. My writing is clay, building from the ground up as I sculpt my way forward until everything has hardened and cooled. Then, I will present myself re-formed to the world. Anna would hate this last sentence.

'Here is the first allusion,' I say to no one in particular.

Music, art, sport. All of them infuse themselves into my story. These are the things we did together. They helped us navigate the world. Everything in front of me now exists as a painting. The blues rushing into the reds, the hiragana melting into the kanji, the advertisements merging into the composed postures. Passengers on this train are quietly inventing new forms of communication as they wordlessly orate with their eyebrows. This brief calm lasts until I get off.

The next stop is Harajuku.

I flick open *Norwegian Wood* as the train slows. I'm reading too much meaning into the chapter headings in the table of contents. Patterns, everywhere. Anna and I always liked puzzles, deciphering clues. As teenagers we would lock ourselves in her parents' garage and listen to obscenely loud music, playing chess, analysing movies and finishing the weekend crossword. There is a comfort in finding order within disarray. Maybe I am trying to find something that isn't there.

I hop off the train, placing the book in the large jacket pocket under my arm, keeping it warm and close.

Beside me is yet another tourist, marvelling over wondrous, small things. 'Doesn't this canned bread look amazing?' she remarks, then disappears with the forward motion of the crowd tumbling into daylight and light rain.

This part of the city is defined by its laneways as much as its open spaces. In a corner market stall, I spot a plastic horse-head mask. I'd love to hide behind the white-cropped mane. With my mask on I could tell passers-by I needed more time to understand Murakami, to figure out the construction of his work; instead, I do the only thing you can do when you don't buy the object you desire—I take a photo of it with my phone for later. For Anna.

I walk past the crêpes and cotton candy. My hair is starting to sulk in all the damp. I am daydreaming about running as I begin to cross the road. A life-size Mario Kart swerves at the traffic lights, missing me by centimetres. *Norwegian Wood* falls out of my jacket and into a puddle, dirtying up the cover and soaking the first few pages.

The tyres of Baby Luigi's car scrape the curb. *'Daijoubu desu ka?* Are you okay?' he asks, at least I think that's what he says—the street noise builds with more and more Mario Karts arriving by the minute. Baby Luigi grimaces as he gets out to check the back wheels. It is completely my fault. He wipes the rain off his face and gives me the thumbs up. I reply with the same gesture, standing there feeling ridiculous. 'You know,' he says, 'you could get very hurt. You must have your eyes open to where you are going!'

I nod. He drives off as suavely as you can with a giant green hat and a low-gravity car. My heart is still pounding as the rain starts up, heavier this time. I pick up my book wrapping it into plastic before placing it carefully inside my bag.

Taking refuge in the bookstore at the edge of the crossing, I check my phone for any news.

'Do you need help? *Nanika osagashi desuka?'* The shop assistant smiles.

'Hai,' I say, still flushed and anxious, staring at the elevation of books. Her name tag says 'Midori' in purple ink and I expect the entire album of *Rubber Soul* to fall down the narrow staircase and consume me. She points me to the fiction.

I want to put my copy of *Norwegian Wood* back on the shelf so someone else can find Murakami, but there are too many notes in the margins, too many stanzas of my own work creased into the edges. My face contorts into an inaudible cry. I stop myself. There's no time for this, not now. I have to find the right book for Anna.

In the short story section, I close my eyes, reach out my hand and take a risk. I pick *Tiny Stories* by Taeko Kono. Her lyrical vignettes are about surprises. I stand there reading the story about a woman who changes into a bird to escape her past—narrative fragments of hope and transformation.

'The way you're standing, so tall and quiet, you look like the grey heron,' says Midori quietly.

I exhale.

'Choose any book in this section. They all have fascinating endings.' Before she completes the last syllable, she disappears behind a black curtain.

Kono's valiant words allow me enough gumption to form coherent words to send to Anna. *I'm not sure I found all I needed to, but you were in everything I was looking at. Home before long I promise. P.S. Murakami's books are heavy.*

Anna writes back. *Time to put Murakami down. Soon, yes, soon.*

I buy the book and make my way to the station, again. This time, heading for the airport, I know everything I need to say and realise how this story will end. I take out my notebook and begin to write.

Moments, splintered in microscale.

The Interview

Jake Dean

Gaz Garret's Northern Rivers home was an hour south of Burleigh. I pretended I wasn't nervous but, as I neared his property, my arms involuntarily swung the steering wheel into the carpark of a macadamia-themed tourist castle. I sipped coffee by the window, looking towards the highway, pulling out my folded list of questions. Cringeworthy. 'What has a life of surfing taught you?' 'Why have you eschewed the limelight?' I paid attention to the questions I'd crossed out: 'What prompted you to disappear? What does one gain?' Double-checking I had spare batteries for the Dictaphone, I tried to remember why I'd wanted to become a surf journalist.

Gaz had once been ubiquitous in surfing. He'd never won a world title but could've nabbed twelve. While his nineteen-seventies counterparts embraced the sport's burgeoning professionalism, Gaz tinkered with things that took his attention away from competition. He experimented with weird cameras, shaped even weirder boards, and wrote magazine columns detailing the labyrinthine mechanics of breaking waves. He invented a long list of manoeuvres, choosing lines on waves no one had even considered. Well into his sixties, he was still performing on par with the current 'world's best'—lithe twenty-somethings sporting ironic haircuts and sponsor logos. Then he all but vanished. The letter that arrived on my editor's desk was the only evidence he hadn't disappeared completely.

As I rounded a bend, I almost missed the dirt track leading to his property. It forged a narrow gap through leering trees as if warding visitors away. I sat idling alongside a rusty red letterbox to check I was in the right place, but my phone had no reception. The rocky track ascended before it reached a small dirt clearing where an old white ute and a squat green shed gathered dust. A narrow, tree-lined bridge crossed a rocky stream to a rustic two-storey timber house. Moss-coated timber and wire handrails clung to stocky timber posts. The deck was illuminated by yellow porch lights, glowing brilliantly amid the dense canopy of rainforest.

While the chances of something happening to me were minuscule, there was something unsettling about Gaz's isolation, the overcast sky and the acid-trip broccoli heads of the trees—so alien to the dry tinderbox foliage back home. I realised I was clutching my keys, a reflex of solo post-nightclub walks, searching for taxis in Surfers Paradise.

I admired his decision to turn away from the world. In many ways, it's what I was doing. I'd chased and accepted a job on the East Coast, packed my entire life into my station wagon and left Adelaide behind—cretinous boys, humdrum days, my dad's domineering bullshit. I felt free when I was alone, surfing back-beaches across the New South Wales border. I came alive when the guys from work left the pub. The night became charged with possibility. Sharks and late-night misogynists be damned. I wanted to know what had pushed Gaz towards *his* solitude. What had festered since?

Another part of me was spiritually drained from being at the magazine. I feared Gaz's story would simply be another in a long line of puff pieces I'd already written, albeit with an astronomically higher profile. All my interview subjects, mostly men, had reached their surfing zenith because it'd been an incurable obsession since they were pre-pubescent, leaving them with very little time for anything else. For all their mastery, I found most devoid of ideas. It was surfing and its nexus with the natural world that interested me, not the brain farts of people that did it well.

These thoughts coalesced as I walked towards the bridge. I resolved that if Gaz's interview hugged familiar terrain, I'd be forced to shake things up. I'd leave the magazine with a bang, whether they published my hit piece or if I was forced to submit it to another publisher.

A screen door shrieked as I reached the stairs and Gaz peered out, freckled head and wild blue hawkish eyes, just like in the magazines and posters. He had a leathery neck, bushy beard, and sun-bleached curls, golden-grey. He looked more like a World War Two deserter than the world's best surfer. He waved awkwardly and I gave him a self-conscious hand flick.

'Meg?' he said, when I reached the deck. He was shirtless and barefoot, wearing threadbare drawstring shorts. At the slightest of movements, muscle fibres sprang to life along his arms and neck, his skin dark as almonds. I was stunned by his lack of body fat.

'Yeah, nice to meet you.' We locked clammy hands, and my heart began beating like I'd spotted a circling fin in the water. We stood there silently, his eyes darting everywhere except towards mine, until he rushed towards the door.

'That'll be the kettle!' he said.

By the time I realised he wanted me to follow him, he was at the sink, stacked haphazardly with dirty dishes.

'So, you're a surf writer?' he shouted over banging cupboards. 'Great gig! Don't be giving that up.' His voice was an octave higher than I'd remembered from his films.

I looked around the living room and kitchen, which had a sweaty smell, and was horrified at the mess covering every surface. Dirty plates, carrot stems, apple cores, piles of notebooks, broken pens, faded T-shirts with holes the size of fifty-cent coins, crude surfboard fins with weird shapes cut out, dog-eared paperbacks. I spied a cute vintage Voigtlander camera fringed by a black banana peel under the coffee table and wondered whether it still worked.

For someone who'd graced more surf magazine covers than anyone alive, I expected there'd be a framed photo, trophy, or magic board he'd ridden during some iconic trip. Instead, the cream walls were bare, except for stains and the odd nail. I only noticed the ancient three-legged blue heeler, lying on a pile of blankets and surrounded by stacks of yellowing newspapers, when it raised its salt-and-pepper head with a tongue-curling yawn.

'Here you go,' Gaz said, suddenly beside me, a mug in his outstretched hand. Steam curled towards my nostrils, and I could immediately tell it was Blend 43, which had probably been calcifying in his pantry for years. I took a sip and burnt my lips so badly I thought they'd blister.

'Mind if I turn this on?' I pulled out my Dictaphone.

'Not at all,' he said, meeting my eyes for the first time. 'Shall we get this show on the road?' He turned towards the door.

I was anxious to start the interview, but it would be on his terms— at least for now. I followed him down the stairs and along a snaking path behind the house, where I ditched my coffee. He walked ahead silently, leading me through a clearing. I spotted a weather-beaten wooden sign fashioned into an arrow and nailed to a tree. It read 'Swimming hole'. For a second, I wondered whether he'd drown me. When we reached a row of trees at the far edge of the clearing, he stopped at the head of a short dirt track that descended sharply to the water's edge.

'Watch your step,' he said. 'Slippery.'

At the bottom, we were shut off from the entire world by trees, as if in a terrarium. A thin timber jetty zig-zagged a few metres into the still-green creek, which was about thirty metres wide. Leaves ebbed on the surface. The 'seeeeep' of a bird pierced the silence.

'Azure kingfisher,' Gaz said, gazing up at the trees.

'What a spot,' I said, transfixed. 'I understand you've lived here your whole life.'

'Yeah, it's all there in Nick Carroll's book.' He slapped a mosquito on his forearm.

I tried to remember the questions I'd written, but his strange, curt responses unnerved me.

'If you don't mind me asking, why am I here if it's all in Nick's biography?'

He sighed and looked towards the middle of the water.

'I want to show you something,' he said.

He tiptoed around the reedy edge of the swimming hole until he reached a break in the foliage. Bending down, he disappeared momentarily, before emerging with a beautiful lipstick-red surfboard.

'Did you wanna have a try?' he said, reappearing at the foot of the jetty.

'Excuse me?'

'Keen for a paddle?'

I searched his eyes and wondered whether he'd ever sought professional help.

'I don't know what you mean.'

'Right, right,' he muttered. Turning his back to me, he walked across the jetty into the middle of the swimming hole. When he reached the end, he threw the board into the water, diving in before climbing onto his board, paddling a few unhurried strokes, and then sitting astride it as if waiting for a wave.

Here comes the hippie shit about being one with the water, I thought. I walked to the jetty's end, knowing whatever happened next would make great copy.

'What kind of waves do you like, Meg?' he asked, suddenly jubilant.

'I'm from Adelaide,' I laughed. 'I'm not picky.'

'Go on, you must have a favourite! Goofy or regular foot?'

'Goofy.'

'Ah, a left-lover. How about a point break? Everyone loves point breaks.'

He closed his eyes and I gasped as the water at the back of the swimming hole began rushing towards him, like someone had pulled a plug. By the time he opened his eyes and lay on his board, the water began curling and bottoming out beneath him. Without paddling, he sprang nonchalantly to his feet. The water's surface morphed into a gorgeous head-high stationary wave, which sent a flurry of squawking birds into the sky.

'The trick with point breaks—with all waves, Meg ...' he shouted above the sound of cascading water, '... is timing, weight transfer, leading with your head and arm. The rest is just noise.'

He bent his knees and compressed his lower body, his back facing the wave, driving towards the flat part of the water. Then, in one rapid yet graceful motion, he looked over his shoulder and pointed his leading left arm towards the wave's crest, his body following the line. The tail of his board gouged the lip at twelve o'clock, sending a white plume of spray into the rainforest. Reaching the trough again, he immediately pumped back towards the lip, this time launching high above the wave, grabbing the board with his left hand as he soared, before reconnecting seamlessly with the water.

His body relaxed as if someone had switched the 'off' button. The wave subsided as quickly as it appeared and he returned to his stomach to ride the final skerrick of whitewater towards me.

'What do you reckon?' he said, joining me on the jetty. Water ran down his body and pooled at his feet.

'What the hell was that?' I asked. My mind was adrift, attempting to compute the ramifications of his invention.

He laughed.

'But how does it do that?' I stammered.

'You don't get it. *I* did that. I think up a wave and it appears.'

I replayed his ride, and it dawned on me—as I considered the wave's imperfections—that he was telling the truth. I'd witnessed something unfathomable, dreamt up by someone, or something, imbued with strange powers.

'I realised I could do it when I was a kid, but only here,' he said.

I knew no synonyms would later do justice to this moment. I checked my Dictaphone to make sure it was still recording. International headlines with my byline flashed before my eyes.

'Why are you showing me this?'

'Well, I had to show *someone*.'

'You've never told anyone?'

'My folks knew, but they died when I was nineteen. I was surfing Sunset. Car crash. No brothers or sisters. I flew home for the funerals and then just surfed here, over and over again. I didn't need anyone else, didn't have to face the grief. I just came here and surfed my brains out. Turned on the happiness tap. I had heaps of mates, but we weren't on the same wavelength. I kept everyone at arm's length. Show them *this*? I thought about winning world titles, even just one, but I don't reckon I could've lived with the guilt.'

He sat down on the jetty and dangled his feet in the water. I sat next to him.

'I know this is a lot. The way I see it, my life has this big asterisk next to it. I just need someone to write the footnote.'

'I'm not gonna write your obituary, Gaz.'

He laughed and flicked a leaf into the creek.

'This past year, all I've wanted to do was disappear and live a simple life someplace else, but this ... thing. It's destroyed me.'

'What do you mean?'

'Imagine you can draw upon ecstasy, dopamine, whenever you want. It mucks up all the levels in there, Meg. I don't find joy in anything anymore, but I'm addicted to coming here all the same.' He rubbed his eyes with his palms.

Was I wasting *my* reservoirs of joy, far from home and those I loved, surfing alone and having bad sex with strangers? I wanted to console him. Tell him his life was worthwhile—anyone in his position would've done the same. Another part of me wanted to tell him his life had indeed been a lie, but there was still no sense in disappearing. It only left you alone and afraid.

I was angry at him for foisting it all on me, but I knew then it was my choice and I wouldn't be the one to tell his story. I didn't want the burden of processing his complex life into a measly three-thousand-word story, only for it to be wrenched away from him and twisted ad nauseam once it hit the news and social media. I couldn't protect him. Maybe no one could.

I thought about Mum, forever in Dad's shadow. I thought about my sister's growing belly. I thought about my best friend and the shitty things I'd said to her before I left. I yearned to return to them—to become the cool auntie I'd always envisaged, be a better friend and daughter, drink cups of tea with them in backyards on lazy afternoons, sitting in green plastic outdoor chairs alongside Besser Block walls and half-dead succulents—leave the glitzy façade of the Gold Coast behind.

'You know, it's only started to occur to me lately that maybe what really matters is the people you surround yourself with. Maybe that's where I went wrong,' he said.

He stood up then, and tossed his board back into the water, before diving in. When he resurfaced, treading water, he was smiling like a boy, gazing up at the trees.

'Everything you need is in the house—videos, journals, whatever you want,' he said.

'Okay,' I said, confused.

'I've read your stuff, Meg. I know you see through the bullshit. That's why I chose you! You're an outsider like me.'

'Because I'm a girl?'

'Because you're from Adelaide.' His weathered face crinkled into a laugh.

'I'm glad to have met you! I'm sorry it had to work out this way, but no one would've believed it otherwise. Look after three-legged Greg for me, will ya?'

The hairs stood up on the back of my neck.

'Gaz, what ...'

He didn't respond. Instead, he climbed back on his board and paddled into the middle of the swimming hole.

'Gaz!'

This time, instead of sitting on his board, he stood, dove off. His feet disappeared, bubbles in his wake.

When he didn't resurface for twenty, then thirty, seconds, I prepared to jump in, but I froze when the jetty began to shake. I scurried to the top of the track and turned to see the water's surface listing again as if a huge wave was forming. Instead, the water rose higher and higher towards the top of the trees. The muddy bottom was filled with rocks, flapping fish, turtles, water dragons, even a platypus, all of them stunned to find themselves submerged in the air alongside a crouching man, dripping with water, head in his hands.

The stunning mass of water was suspended thirty metres above the ground when I realised what he was planning, only before I could do anything, the spell broke. The water dropped with the weight of a small ocean, and I closed my eyes to brace for impact.

Clocks

Joshua Baird

At exactly midnight, Henry was born. Curled and warm in a dark balloon, he didn't want to leave so the obstetrician used a vacuum to pull him out headfirst. He was pink, slimy, swollen, wretched, and he cried until he was placed in the nook of his mother's arm. She traced a gentle finger around the raised red ring that the vacuum left on the top of her only child's head. He stretched his little arms and toes, closed his fingers around things that touched his palms, wrinkled his nose and opened his mouth in a misshapen 'O' when he yawned, unaware that after so little time he was already adored. Everything was perfect; nothing was out of place. He slotted nicely between his mother and father, filling a once empty space the exact shape of his tiny body.

At five he had read every book he owned and, because they had no others, he began to read his mother's recipe books. His mother and father proudly told their friends about how much Henry read, about how rather than reading books out loud to him, *Henry* would read to *them*.

'Four sprigs of fresh ...' he paused, unfamiliar with the next word. He pronounced it with the hissing 'th' sound at the beginning. '*Thime?*'

'T-yme,' his mother corrected, the tip of her tongue tapping the roof of her mouth behind her teeth to make a 't' sound. 'Thyme.'

'Thyme.' The sound entered the vastness of his mind, where all the things he learned accumulated, sorted themselves into neat stacks, and stayed there forever.

At nine, his reports showed that he excelled in reading and writing, but he displayed a particular flair for mathematics. During tests, he took his time. While other students rose and handed their papers to the teacher, he checked and re-checked his answers, keeping his eye on the clock, ensuring that he used every minute.

At a parent-teacher interview, his teacher smiled across the table at his mother and father who sat on either side of Henry.

'You have a genius on your hands,' she said.

'I thought we might,' his mother replied.

'If you keep this up,' the teacher continued, looking at Henry now, 'you might become a world-renowned mathematician.'

The word 'mathematician', longer than some entire sentences, took shape in his brain, the letters falling into place next to one another, the familiar 'th' hissing sound eventually followed by the ever-deceptive letter 'c' in place of a 'sh', a lesson on the refusal of the English language to follow any set of unbreakable rules. When he arrived home, he wrote the word in his journal and noticed how none of its thirteen letters dipped below the line.

At seventeen, it was time to choose. His numerical brain had surpassed those of his teachers, and he had received letters inviting him to study maths at several universities. When he read their invitations, the words rearranged themselves on the page, each sentence flowing more naturally, more beautifully into the next.

When he told his parents that he'd chosen to study writing, not maths, at university, he detected a tinge of consternation, a moment of surprised hesitation in their expressions. But perhaps he was projecting the thoughts of his worried mind onto their faces.

'I'm glad. Do what you love,' his father said, his mouth hidden by a beard.

'It's wonderful that you're following your heart, darling,' his mother said, her smile lifting the bags beneath her eyes.

Their words danced in circles in his brain.

His money ran low so he took a job working three days a week as a clerk at a clock store. Clocks covered every wall's surface, and as he stood behind the desk waiting for customers who rarely came, hundreds of clocks tick, tick, ticked, all out of time with each other. His days passed slowly because he could never forget the time; there was always a clock nearby to remind him.

He came to know the faces of clocks better than his own. Over time, he developed two astounding skills: he could tell you the exact time down to the minute at any point in the day; and, assisted by his prodigious maths skills, he could instantaneously convert any period of time into hours, minutes, and seconds. Nine hours became thirty-two thousand, four hundred seconds. One hundred years became eight hundred and seventy-six thousand hours, plus leap days.

I've been working for five hours, twenty-six minutes, and four seconds, he thought, *which means there are three hours, thirty-three minutes, and fifty-four seconds before I finish my shift.*

When he closed his eyes at night, he saw the clocks' faces and heard them tick.

At twenty-one, the year he started writing a PhD thesis on the theme of time in literature, he met Hannah, a first-year nursing student. With a plastic-wrapped sandwich in his hand, he stood in the university cafeteria looking for an empty table. There came a girl's voice that said, 'You can sit here' and he turned to find Hannah, whose name he didn't know yet. Stupidly, he almost declined, not wanting to be a burden.

He took the seat and saw that she wore a sweater striped with each colour of the rainbow. The sun had sprinkled a few soft freckles across her nose. Her auburn-dyed hair was tied up in a ponytail. 'So it doesn't get in the way when I take notes,' she told him. He would later see her let it down at night countless times. She had lived in London after school and returned a year ago to study nursing. She worked part-time pouring wine at a French restaurant. When she spoke, she cast her eyes down as if deciding between two answers to a question. When she listened, she gazed straight into his eyes.

By the time he loved her, he knew that she read gothic horror novels under the morning sun. When she was cold, she preferred to turn the heater on than to wear a jumper. She never liked a song until she knew what it was about. She liked to be alone during the daytime, but once night came, she needed him near. She was filled with love, loved to love, to be loved, and was easily hurt by acts of unloving. She arched her back when his fingers brushed the skin that covered her spine.

On a picnic blanket, only a few months after they met, with a cheese platter and the city spread out before them, she told him that this was her idea of bliss. 'Just you and me and food,' she said. 'We don't even have to talk.' They listened to the birds and the distant traffic.

They were both twenty-one, born on the same day of the same year. When they met, they thought it was some colossal coincidence. By the time they were in love, they thought it must mean something, like the world had entwined them, tangled vines slowly crawling up a trellis.

At twenty-three, he and Hannah moved into a two-bedroom unit next to the clock store. The house stood rigid, bearing no expression, feeling nothing for the two standing before it. It wasn't where they wanted to be, but it was a stepping stone while Henry completed his thesis. Time would bring something better.

The little garden at the front of the house was already dying when they moved in. It was a shamble of sickly dark green leaves and red petals that drooped, roused lazily by the breeze. Plastic bags and food wrappings blown in from the street seemed to choke the garden at its roots.

Inside the house, there were dents and scratches on the walls from previous owners. The rooms had looked spacious when Henry and Hannah had inspected the house, but once they'd moved their furniture in, the rooms felt smaller, as if the walls had closed in around their things to take a closer look.

Whenever Hannah had a bad day, Henry would take her in his arms and together they would look at their things. The fruit bowl. Her paintings. The fiddle-leaf fig that touched the ceiling. 'This is ours,' Henry would say.

The study was cluttered with piles of Henry's books and was where he spent most of his time. One more year of study, then he'd get a higher-paying job and they could move somewhere else.

At night, through the closed bedroom window, he could hear the ticking of the clocks next door.

Hannah quit her studies and worked full time pouring wine at the restaurant to keep money in their bank account. Like Henry, her job gave rise to certain talents. No matter who you were, she could find you the perfect wine. She would talk with you, learn about you, and at some sudden point in the conversation, she'd say, 'I've got it.' And then she'd come back and pour a glass, and it would be your new favourite wine. Each time, as the liquid passed through the bottle's neck, it was as if she could feel, deep within herself, the filling of the glass, the vanishing of empty space.

She worked nights, but when she was at home, she knew better than to disturb Henry while he wrote. Ten, twenty, thirty times a day she walked past the closed study door. Occasionally she stopped and quietly pressed her ear against it, listening for the absence of movement inside.

He knew she was there. He could hear her silence and see the shadows of her feet under the door. He knew exactly how many times per day she passed the door and how many times she stopped; he'd been watching, listening, counting. It was a pleasant digression from the blank white stare of his computer screen and the expectant blink of the cursor.

At thirty-three, it was time to choose. They had spoken about children before but the conversations made Henry impatient.

'Let's not talk about that now,' he'd said. 'I'll finish my thesis, get a proper job, and then we can talk about kids.' He'd learned to shape his tone into a full stop.

But he heard it in his own voice. Every year was the year he'd finish.

She startled him when she opened the study door. They talked, and by the time she left the room, they'd agreed: instead of having children, they'd focus on their careers—his then hers.

'Remember?' Henry said. 'Your idea of bliss?'

As Hannah walked down the corridor away from the study, Henry felt the growing of a space between them, its shape indefinable. He turned back to the screen.

At forty-one, he spent an entire year lying on the floor. His thesis stopped still and he needed time to think, so he asked for a year off from the clock store and laid his body on the carpet in the study, his arms and legs spread like a starfish, and listened to the ticking of the clocks next door. Three times a day, Hannah brought him meals. At night, he wouldn't come to bed. He remained on the floor of the study where he slept. He refused to move. He was growing old, stagnant. An undiscovered pond with nothing growing inside.

At forty-two, he peeled himself off the floor and went back to his job, three days a week.

At fifty, he felt that over the twenty-eight years, four months, two weeks, and four days he'd been writing his thesis, the more he researched and wrote about time, the more his thesis felt like a dark corridor, an open doorway with the light shining through like a distant star at the end. He could never tell if he was getting closer to the door; it was entirely possible that he was getting further away. He was weary. It seemed he had spent most of his life looking out the study window at a dying garden. He owed half a lifetime to Hannah. At all times during the twenty-nine years they had known each other, his mind had been in front of the computer screen, thinking of the next word.

Hannah often went out in the evening to see her friends. Henry barely spoke anymore, and his company was no longer enough.

'I just want to *talk* to you,' Hannah pleaded one night as Henry sat stupidly with a fork in one hand and a knife in the other. 'To *converse*. I want you to say something meaningful. Even if you just pretend there is something you'd like to tell me about. Whatever it is, I'll listen.'

He tried to think of something to say. After a silence, he moved to the study and closed the door, where his thoughts filled the room and swarmed around him.

If I write ten words a day, he thought, I'll be finished in thirteen years. I'll finish by the time I'm sixty-four.

He placed his fingertips on the keys of the keyboard and searched his mind for ten words.

At sixty-four, he still hadn't finished.

At sixty-seven, his parents died on the same day, lying in the same bed, both of natural causes. It wasn't clear who had died first, but when she heard, Hannah said, 'I guess one couldn't go on living without the other. What a beautiful way to leave the world, together. Like fate.'

To Henry, it was a coincidence.

While emptying his parents' house of its possessions, he found an old notebook of his, and on a page near the beginning, alone, in neat, looping cursive, the word 'mathematician'. He whispered it to himself, admired its syllables, the way that none of its thirteen letters dipped below the line.

He imagined another lifetime where he had chosen to become a mathematician, a prodigy at a young age. In his mind, his life rewound itself. The clocks in the clock store ticked backwards, their arms moving counter-clockwise. The wrinkles on his face smoothed out. He walked backwards from the study and sat at the dinner table across from Hannah, who spoke backwards. At a French restaurant, wine leapt out of glasses and back through the neck of the bottle in Hannah's hand. She started reading gothic horror again, beginning at the back of the book and finishing at the front, lying under a morning sun that moved from west to east. They took all their things from every room, put them back in the car, and reversed away from the house. After they left, the garden slowly came back to life. He lived at his parents' house, she lived at hers. They fell backwards into youth.

He deleted words from the computer screen. His mind cast back in time, as far as it could go, but it couldn't bring itself to rewind past the moment he had met Hannah. Over and over again, in his mind, she said, 'You can sit here,' backwards then forwards, backwards then forwards, like a needle retracing the same spot on a record.

He tried to rewind to the time when he had made his choice, when he had begun writing a thesis on time and literature. But to get there, he had to go back past meeting Hannah. And if he did, if he went back to the point in time before he began to write his thesis, before his choice between words and mathematics, would he find Hannah again? Or would he arrive at the university cafeteria to find that she's nowhere to be seen, their paths uncrossed forever?

He read it over and over again, 'mathematician', the infinite possibilities that lay there within the word. He thought of burning the notebook but, instead, he closed it and put it back where it belonged, in the wardrobe of his old bedroom for someone else to find.

At eighty, he was an old car that never started, covered in dust. There was an engine built inside him for a specific purpose, never realised. Having lain dormant for a lifetime, he feared something in him had corroded. He was unusable; he had missed his chance.

He sat at the computer and a word would come to him once, maybe twice per day. On the rare occasion that he spoke, the words came to him slowly and he placed them carefully like dominoes, one at a time.

The clocks at work had changed; the numbers and hands on their faces were replaced with another language, something foreign that he couldn't grasp. The clocks no longer ticked, and the store was now filled with silence. But Henry felt every second as it passed. He still knew how far he was into his shift and how long left. He knew that his boss, Sylvia—who was his original boss's granddaughter, inheriting the business after her grandfather and father retired— longed to fire him. He was a slow worker who rarely got anything done, and he was driving away customers who grew impatient with his slow, laboured manner of speech.

'When do you think you'll retire, Henry?' she once said. 'Do you think it's time?'

He inhaled deeply like he always did before he spoke, as if he was about to dive underwater.

'As ... time ... passes ... me ... by ...'

She nodded along with his words, wishing she hadn't spoken.

'I ... find ... that ...' He seemed to have forgotten he was speaking to her, instead speaking to the clocks now, his eyes searching them as if he found the words on their faces. 'Were ... it ... not ... for ... this ... job ...'

'It's alright,' Sylvia said, but he didn't seem to hear her.

'And ... these ...'

'It's fine, Henry,' she said. 'You have a job here as long as you're willing.'

'Clocks ...'

She left the room. The words still came to him slowly, but no one heard them.

At one hundred, Hannah died with Henry at her side. Her friends and family members, great-nephews and great-nieces and first cousins twice removed, people that Henry didn't recognise, gathered in the room. He was glad that it wasn't among the wired machines and whiteness of a hospital but in their home with people she apparently loved.

But at the very instant that the final breath slipped from her lungs, and he was left sitting beside her, he realised there was an expanse that separated him from Hannah, even now. He felt the empty space in the room, its form imperceptible, and knew that now she was gone the space couldn't be filled.

The wound of Hannah's death remained; Henry ran his finger along it every day, refusing to let it heal. Even worse was the empty space, which before he only felt in Hannah's presence, or when she lingered outside the study door. It now lingered at the front of his mind like a tumour behind his eyes.

My ... whole ... life ... he thought. *My ... whole ... life.*

Though the words came slowly, they did come. He could feel the end now, coming closer every day.

He began to put the finishing touches on his thesis. He looked out past the computer screen, out the study window. The garden stooped towards the ground, and Henry marvelled at how he'd never done a thing to maintain it, yet it remained insistently alive.

body of work

Sarah Giles

My backpack's still on my shoulders. I take it off and hold it to my chest, but it feels childish, so I set it down by my feet. I don't know what to do with my hands. Clasped feels formal, arms-crossed feels cold, resting on my knees is too open and could be unsustainable as my anxiety rises. I opt for palm-to-palm, clamped between my knees. I think this will make me look still and casual, comfortable even. I am compact and in control of my body.

It's a patchwork loungeroom. None of the furniture matches and I wonder if that's a deliberate choice or a simple share house standard. The couch I'm sitting on is covered in tasselled pillows and crocheted throws, a mix of bright colours. Then there's a firm-looking armchair with square wooden armrests and aggressive red upholstery. Next to that is a wingback chair, threadbare green velvet with a couple of patches on its arms. There's no TV, which I love, and there's a long glass and timber cabinet with bottles of alcohol on top, sitting among lush green plants. There are board games stuffed in the shelf space below.

I hear footsteps and pinch my hands tight between my knees.

'Clair this is June and Luca,' Nadia says, flopping on the couch next to me.

June has a slick, black pixie haircut and big, leopard print glasses. She shakes my hand and sits on the firm red chair, crossing her legs, hands on knees. Luca has brown skin and a buzzcut. He sits in the wingback chair, glancing at me for a second before becoming fascinated with his fingernails. Luca wears glasses too but they're wire-rimmed and almost invisible. Nadia sits on the couch sideways, facing me, and folds a leg beneath her. She leans back into the armrest, flinging an arm over the back of the couch.

'About the room,' Nadia says. 'It's five-fifty a month, utilities and all that included. Internet too. It's furnished with a double mattress, a chest of drawers and a desk. And plenty of room for an easel, I know you're an artist.'

'Good to know,' I nod, 'but I don't have an easel anymore.'

'What happened to it?' Luca says.

I want to clench my hands. 'Had to leave it behind.'

He looks back down at his hands and I notice he's trying to scrape paint flecks off his fingers. 'I've got a spare you can use.'

Nadia brings us back to business.

'You'll pay for your own groceries and one night a week you'll cook for us. We take turns. You'll wanna be home for June's night, she's a chef.'

'Apprentice,' June says. 'But yeah, an above-average apprentice. Where do you work?'

'Just started at a restaurant on Acland.'

June looks at Nadia for a moment and shakes her head.

'We don't discriminate against people because they work in an insecure industry,' Nadia says. 'You're in hospo too for Christ's sake.'

'Whatever, so long as she pays,' June says. 'Sorry, but I can't afford to cover for another flake.'

Nadia rolls her eyes and turns to me.

'I've got an interview lined up for a second job,' I lie.

'See, she's good for it,' Nadia squeezes my thigh and smiles.

Luca shifts in his seat.

My first night in the share house is a loud one. Nadia's hanging strings of coloured lights around the kitchen ceiling, while June and Luca play cards and drink Tequila and orange juice. I offered to cook, wanting to prove that I'm no freeloader, so the sound of cupboards creaking open and snapping shut adds to the symphony as I search for pots and plates and strainers.

'What's for dinner?' June says.

'Baked potatoes. Nearly ready,' I say, placing a steaming bowl of mixed veggies on the table next to a dish of butter and another of sour cream.

'Fuck yes,' she says.

Luca makes me a gin and tonic as we sit down to eat. He puts it on the table between us.

'Thanks,' I say.

He smiles and picks up a fist-sized potato still wrapped in foil, dropping it onto his plate with a thump.

'They're hot,' I say.

'Yeah,' he says, shaking his hand.

'Dickhead.' June uses the tongs to pick up a potato. 'Clair, so. Where'd you come from?'

Nadia gasps, tying her long curly hair back with a pink satin scrunchie. 'You don't have to answer that.'

'It's okay.' I take a sip of my drink and the lime juice conjures the taste of Candice. 'A town in the Northeast, close to the border.'

'Why'd you leave?' June says.

I take a long pull from my glass, almost draining it. Then, still not sure how to answer, I shrug. Pathetic. 'Did you grow up in Melbourne?' I ask.

'Not really.'

'Yes, you did. You grew up in Bayswater in a house your parents owned,' Nadia says.

'Well, yeah. But that's not *Melbourne*, Melbourne,' June says.

Nadia rolls her eyes.

'What about you two?' I say.

'I'm from Newcastle,' Nadia says. 'Luca's rural too, Shepparton yeah?'

'Basically,' he says. 'Mooroopna.'

We eat quietly for a while. Nadia turns up the music when If Tomorrow Never Comes plays and starts singing along. I make another gin and finish it quickly.

Later, in the lounge, I'm feeling tipsy after another two drinks. The room swirls around us. I want to press my skin against someone else's. The others debate loudly around me, but I'm not listening. I'm fantasising about Candice's hands, about her mouth sucking, pulling at me. She likes to bite me, leaving teeth marks on my skin. I let her do it because afterwards she brushes her fingertips over all the red spots, kissing them gently.

'Hello, Clair.' June is waving her hand in front of my face and I wonder why she keeps saying my name when she speaks to me.

'Sorry.' I blink back into the room.

'I was just saying, how does someone move to a new city with a backpack and no plan?' June pours out shots of Southern Comfort. 'Like, were you homeless or something?'

'What the fuck?' Luca says, picking up a shot glass.

'No judgement. Just asking the question,' she says, downing her liquor.

I look to Nadia for help but she's waiting for my answer too, smiling, and I realise that she is just as nosey as June but not as bold.

'I suppose I ran away.' I take my shot—it's hot and honeyed. 'I'm not a good person.'

'Were you living with your parents?' Nadia asks.

'Girlfriend.'

'She's supportive?' Nadia rests her hand on my knee and I want to spread my legs for her but cross them instead. 'Of the move?'

I shrug.

June starts to nod, knowingly. 'She was abusive.'

'No. Fuck.' I lean back and cover my face with both hands.

Music hums, tuneless house music with heavy bass that pulses in my gut over and over and over, and it feels as if it flows beneath us like water under a bridge.

'I left a note on the kitchen table,' I say, wiping a couple of selfish tears away.

'Oh, I didn't see it,' Luca says, moving to get up.

'No. At home.' My head's warm, swimming. 'I ran away.'

The sobs are thick, getting trapped in my throat, escaping as painful moans.

Luca pours me another shot and wraps my hand around it. 'It'll help.'

'I'm fucking terrible,' I say. 'I love her but it's really hard.'

'Drink,' he says.

We all drink.

I wake up on the couch, a pair of calloused feet in my face. Nadia is splayed out next to me. Luca sleeps neatly in his armchair, arms crossed, forehead pressed against the wing part of the wingback. I can't see June. I climb over Nadia and head into the backyard.

The share house has a courtyard. I sit at a scrappy wooden table watching a sparrow hop across the garden bed, pecking at the dirt, hopping some more. I take a dinner plate from inside and fill it with water, then nestle it in the garden a little away so I don't spook the bird. When Dad got his own place out of town, he hung bird feeders from the low-hanging tree branches and spent a weekend making a couple of birdhouses out of greying timber sleepers that were dug out of disused train tracks at the outskirts. He painted them in bright colours and, when I came to visit, we'd take chairs from the kitchen into the yard to watch the birds.

From the table in the courtyard, I watch the sparrow skip closer to the plate and, eventually, she flutters into the puddle, dropping her beak to take a sip. Her fragile neck bends back to swallow and then she dips her head again, wetting her feathers.

I draw my hand up to my neck, giving it a squeeze. Tension shoots up the back of my scalp, my pulse pushing against my fingers. Tendons roll under my skin. I read somewhere that it takes almost five minutes to die from manual strangulation but only a few seconds to lose consciousness. I squeeze harder, feeling the blood pound behind my eyes. The sun is too bright and I know I don't have the strength and that my body will never submit. When I release myself, a heavy blackness momentarily obscures my vision and, like standing up too quickly, I become lightheaded.

The bird is gone and the sun has drifted behind a cloud.

Nadia comes by work at closing and takes me to a bar down the street. She buys us two gin cocktails and when I ask how much they cost so I can pay her back she tells me not to worry.

'It's on my boyfriend,' she says, flashing a metallic credit card.

We grab a booth by the open window where the breeze is cool and musky. The smell of weed wafts in and Nadia takes a deep breath. The cocktail tastes sour and chemically. Nadia says it's because it was made with bottled lime juice.

'I'm going to transfer you some cash,' I say.

'Don't even.'

I open my bank app. 'I'll just send it to the rent account?'

Nadia slaps her hand on the table between us, laughing at the loud snapping sound it makes. 'Please,' she says. 'Just let me pay for it.'

The glow of my phone screen lights us up from below. I'm frowning as Nadia takes it, locks it and puts it back on the table.

'It's on me tonight. Well, on him.' She sips, wrinkling her nose. 'Fuck, this is filthy.'

I decide it would be more awkward to press the money thing than to just let her shout me this time. 'Tell me about your boyfriend.'

'This one,' she smiles, patting her wallet, 'is only in Melbourne a couple of nights a month. He has one of me in every city.'

Since moving to Melbourne, I have been frequently reminded of how small my world is. I nod. 'Is it a job, or ...'

'Kind of?' She bobs her head from side to side. 'Actually, no. He's just a generous guy who travels a lot and hates sleeping alone. My main partner, Jaz, travels for work too. He spends one month working in the mines and then he gets a week home with me.'

'Don't you miss him?'

Nadia sips her drink, nods, then sips again. 'Yes and no. I prefer the space, so does he.'

'Does he ... sorry. Is it okay to ask questions?'

Nadia sweeps her hand, palm up, between us.

'Does he sleep with other people, too?'

'Yeah, a month is a fucking long time to go without.' Nadia cackles into her drink.

'Do you get jealous?'

'Nah, I want him to be happy. I also want me to be happy.'

The image of Candice kissing a disembodied someone floats into my head. They reach for each other, pulling close, and soon Candice's worn-out underwear that she refuses to replace is hanging from one ankle.

'I don't think I couldn't handle it.'

'It's not for everyone.' Nadia shrugs. 'What's the story with your partner?'

'Candice,' I say, feeling the alcohol softening my tongue.

I'm still one foot in the fantasy, sliding Candice's underwear onto the floor, reaching my hand up her calf, thigh, her stomach. We kiss. I ignore the other woman going down on her.

'It's messy,' I say.

The bar is crowded now—voices curdle around us and we have to shout to be heard. We've settled into our booth. Nadia had emptied the contents of her bag while searching for her Chapstick and now we're surrounded by crumpled notepads, pens, tampons, condoms, loose change, a bent copy of *In My Skin* and a red velour scarf that she tied around my wrist after I said it was soft.

'Are you afraid to say it out loud? Nadia's holding my hand and looking at me through shiny brown eyes.

'Afraid to say what?' I ask.

'That you're mad and you're hurt,' she says.

Something sharp pierces my stomach and I try to pull my hand away, but Nadia holds me tight. The loose tassels of the scarf trail across her hands. It looks like we've tied ourselves together.

'It's okay to be mad at her. You can tell me. I won't repeat it.'

Nadia crosses her heart with her free hand. I think about being mad at Candice. It feels ludicrous.

'I abandoned her. Went back on my word after saying I'd support her, after telling her we'd be alright. She didn't do anything.' I chew the inside of my cheek. 'It doesn't feel fair to be mad.'

'Why?' Nadia punctuates her question with a squeeze of my hand.

'Because I'm the one who fucked up.'

She tugs on the end of the red scarf. 'We all fuck up.'

The next morning, I sleep late and when I stumble into the kitchen a little before noon, I find Luca staring into space, gripping a mug of green tea with both hands.

'You draw?' Luca asks.

I shrug, nod.

'Me too,' he says. 'I paint.'

'Yeah. I paint as well, with ink mostly.'

'There's this thing on today. I usually go with someone but it's weird between us right now. I've never gone alone.'

Luca is turning the mug in his hands and staring into the gently lapping water inside.

'Are you inviting me?'

'Yeah,' he says.

I take my cup of tea into the bathroom where I shower and brush my teeth, leaving the house with hair still damp and my tea forgotten on the windowsill above the sink.

We catch the 67 tram towards the city, sitting quietly, our thighs touching. Luca tells me when to get up and I follow him into the Royal Botanic Gardens. My canvas bag bounces off my hip. Inside is my sketchbook, a pot of Indian ink, paintbrushes and some folded-up paper towels.

'What exactly is this thing?' I say.

'It's a club for shy artists.' He checks his phone for the exact location of the meet-up.

We hike up a hill and spot a scattered group of people sitting in the grass, each bent over their laps, scribbling away. I watch a couple of other latecomers walk from the opposite direction and sit at the farthest outskirts of the group. Luca finds a wide clearing and lays out the quilt he's taken from his bed. We settle beside each other; Luca fills a palette with various shades of green and yellow and pink paints, pouring water from his drink bottle into a couple of plastic cups. He starts work on an A5 canvas without glancing at me. I look around, amazed at the broad group of artists around us. Painting and drawing in pen, pencil, crayon, charcoal. Candice would love this, though I would never describe her as 'shy'. Pencil shavings blow across the grass towards us, soon picked up by a gust of wind that rustles everyone's paper and lifts the shavings into the air.

My sketchbook is almost full, but I find a clean page and balance the pot of ink on the side of my folded knee. The paint brushes I've brought with me are new, the bristles soft, clean sable hair that glide silky ink lines across the page. It was indulgent, buying new brushes. I'd left my old synthetic ones in the studio because Candice was in there, and I was too much of a coward to face her.

Later, as the group starts to dwindle and the sun dims, Luca asks how I'm doing. I flip my book towards him, showing him a figure crouched in profile but looking forward, mushrooms sprouting from their back and arms and head. Luca lets me see his painting of pink roses, chunky paint punctuating textured leaves, adding depth to the shadows beyond the stems and petals.

We walk back down the hill. The sun has dipped behind the trees. I shiver when the breeze picks up behind us.

'I need to find a place for this,' he says, gingerly holding the canvas.

'Where do you normally keep them?'

'I don't,' he says.

Luca tells me that he leaves his shy artist club pieces in the gardens for someone to find and keep. We walk around the gardens a little while longer, until Luca leaves the painting on a bench seat next to a pond. He takes a photo of it and posts it to an Instagram account with more than sixty thousand followers.

'Are you a big deal?'

Luca shrugs, laughing. 'Don't tell anyone.'

My phone buzzes under my pillow and I answer it without checking to see who's calling.

'Hello?'

I hear muffled swearing.

'Sorry. You were sleeping,' Candice says.

'Hey.' I sit up, wide awake. 'How are you?'

My mouth is sticky and dry. I guzzle water from the cup on my bedside table.

'This feels weird. I shouldn't have called.'

I listen to her breath travelling down the line. 'It's nice to hear from you.'

She grumbles a little. 'Same.'

I imagine her sitting on the couch in the studio in that oversized T-shirt smudged with so much paint that it's hard to tell it used to be white. Her hair's most likely tied back in the frizzy braid she slept in. She's probably drinking her second tea of the morning.

'I've been working at IGA,' she says.

I roll over to face the window. The sun glows behind the curtains. 'Yeah?'

'This woman came in last night wanting to return a pair of sunglasses, so I scanned them in and realised we don't sell them. I told her as much and she insisted she bought them at our store and wanted her money back.'

'Fucking hell.' I sigh.

I slide out of bed and open the curtains. The sky is a perfect pale blue.

'What did you do?' I ask.

'Told her no. She cracked the shits with me, asked for my supervisor.'

'Did they back you up on it?'

'Yeah, absolutely. The woman had a full-on tantrum. We had to have her removed from the store. She was still outside when I finished work,' she says softly. 'And she was crying.'

It's quiet in my room. The clock ticking in the lounge just outside my room sounds abnormally loud.

'She said she was sorry but needed money. I think she's an addict,' Candice says.

'What happened then?'

'Asked her if she'd sell me the sunglasses. Said I really liked them. Then she hugged me, and I started crying too.'

The first thing I think to say is, *That's why I love you.*

'How are you?' she says.

'Busy. Been working at a joint here. It's way busier than I'm used to.'

A strange silence passes between us.

'You're staying then.'

I swallow.

'Are we broken up?' she says.

Nadia's red velour scarf is on my bedside table and I grab it and rub it against my cheek. It's soft like the inside of Candice's thighs and red like her hair. I want to stuff it in my mouth and choke on it. 'I'm sorry.'

Covidiot

Rafael Fajer

I wake up this morning to read the posts on New York Writers Workshop. I come across Rohinton's troubling entry about life in Singapore during the pandemic and how some people still refuse to wear masks. He calls them 'covidiots'. Genius.

It's 5:30 am as I walk to the clinic where I was in rehab for almost a year and in which I am a counsellor. The air is surprisingly brisk and still. The waves of the Pacific Ocean are barely audible. My brain is still soggy from the effects of the antipsychotics I take every night. I'm thinking about what Rohinton's written and how covidiots and their choices affect us all. I live in Tijuana, one of the pandemic's epicentres. Many people here have no government help, no savings, no insurance. They must work. They go out and sell on the streets, in markets, in the 'informal' economy: without permits, outside of the banking system. Most of the stands I visit sell masks, yet the sellers don't wear them. There are no bathrooms around where the sellers are active. People often urinate and defecate on empty lots. I don't see any soap, water, or hand sanitiser on or near their stands. My worries multiply. To add to this problem, those who work in such markets don't have access to healthcare systems.

Near the end of the avenue, where the stands end, I smell some fresh *atole* fumes coming from a hot pot. The vendor is wearing a mask. This is good. I go to him and buy a steaming cup of the brew and say gracias. Meaning 'thank you for this delicious beverage and for wearing a mask'.

How am I participating in the pandemic? I wonder as I sip from the cup. Am I helping? Hindering? At first glance I think about how I'm taking care of myself and others around me by following the instructions of experts: wearing masks, avoiding contact, washing hands, staying in as much as possible, keeping a safe distance, avoiding sex without barriers. I feel like I'm doing well. Am I?

I finish my *atole* as I get to the rehab building. The residents are doing yoga. I check my email while I wait for them to finish. I find a few missives regarding investments I hold. I'm a minor stockholder in all of them, and by 'minor' I mean I have less than 2 per cent in them. For the past two months I've been informed of how, due to the economic hardships of the pandemic, all these enterprises 'have been obligated' to let go of a great number of workers.

My mind turns to the stands selling food and other consumables on the street. The competition is fierce, and it has been growing steadily in recent weeks. This is one of the effects of increased unemployment due to the pandemic. Many have had to turn to this type of work, in the hopes of keeping their families with a roof over their heads and fed.

Then my mind turns to Lola, a counsellor with whom I've become good friends. Her house was burgled yesterday while she was at work. She lives alone and has been working hard to add furniture and appliances to her home. She lost everything when she was in active addiction. Her family, who did not have much to fall back on, disowned her. After living on the streets for a couple of years turning tricks, a friend of hers offered to help her through rehab. She became staff when she left rehab. Staff don't get paid much here. It took her a good three years to manage to buy a couch, a bed, a TV, a speaker, a microwave, a washing machine and a dryer. All the burglars left were the couch and the bed. They even took her clothes.

There has been an uptick in robberies and thefts in Mexico since the pandemic started.

Drug trafficking and use have increased too. Being cooped up with a bunch of people, family or not, is stressful. Especially when you don't know when your next meal will be or if you will have enough for your whole family. Drug-related violence is also on the rise. Competition is growing among cartels; the number of people trying to participate in that market is growing. Having no opportunities for work in factories or restaurants or anywhere else, people are finding it necessary to distribute drugs to make ends meet. And people without anything else to do but worry about how they're going to survive are turning more often than before to drug use. As the demand increases, the employment opportunities do as well. The pandemic is a profitable time for those in the business of drugs.

Prostitution is also more prevalent right now. An increasing number of people need to sell their bodies to gain sustenance. With more people in the prostitution market and less money circulating on the streets, those who are offering up their bodies in this way must do so for a fraction of what they would have been able to make before the pandemic.

Children are dropping out of school to work. There is no money for health care, no employee health insurance. The repercussions are endless, and I worry about how I am contributing to these.

Though I'm doing full-time voluntary service at the clinic, I have investments that are, due to the pandemic (and capitalism, from which I benefit), contributing to the pain and suffering in the world.

I wish I could write that I have a plan, a way out or a way to help, but I don't. I just have this sense that I could be contributing more, that I could be doing better. There's little I can do to get those who have been fired from the businesses where I have investments work but I can do what I am doing today, here at the clinic and in my little corner of the world.

The residents finish their yoga session. We have breakfast and then I lead them in a Guided Imagery through Music session. When we're done, I walk towards the market stand and get a second cup of hot *atole*. This is good.

I think I'll bring my Bluetooth speaker tomorrow, for Lola. Covidiot.

Cheese and Gherkin With
the Crusts Cut Off

Bec Curtin

Grandpa's wig was a carnival. A pink storm of fairy floss. A cyclone of marshmallows. The stiff straw feeding irritated camels.

For years, he'd worn the hairpiece with its pastel shades mirroring the Esperance salt lakes. Mother called Granny cheap for buying the synthetic sort.

But Ellie thought money never seemed short. At her grandparents' house the lace-covered table was piled high with food. Sunny, the cat, hissed at the visitors from a velvet pillow. A pool table in the back room and a fridge that made ice. Push one button and fresh cubes just plopped into your juice. The magic was instant; Ellie felt the thrill rush through her stomach.

All that and a pink wig sitting stoically on Grandpa's head as they visited each Sunday.

'Don't eat the food,' Ellie's mother warned on the drive over.

'Leave it, Julie.' Father scratched the stubble on his chin.

Julie twirled her gold ring, fingernails glinting. 'It's not you she makes the comments to, Matt.'

Their quarrel descended into harsh whispers.

Ellie's sister bumped her shoulder, breathing beneath the radio's spell. 'Remember the lyrics to the song we wrote?'

Ellie's fringe danced from side to side.

'Wanna write more?' Ash asked.

They washed away the world with fantastical teenage drama.

Grandpa met them at the edge of the steep driveway, which curved up to his castle. A faint breeze pushed at the edge of his wig. Smiling distantly, he leant on a walking cane.

Ellie waved to the hairpiece. It waved back.

Granny bustled about the kitchen, a red sheen glossing her lips. She smoothed out invisible crinkles in the tablecloth. Light dripped off the crystal earrings dangling to her shoulders.

'Julie, you've arrived. Hopefully, the pastries aren't ruined,' Granny said in greeting.

She hugged Ellie's father tightly. Toyed with a strand of Ash's golden lion's mane.

'Your hair's gotten long.' Ash preened as Granny continued, 'Julie, you might want to invest in a better-quality conditioner.'

Ellie's mother nodded. Grandpa had followed them up the driveway and into the kitchen. He poured Julie a glass of wine, the tremble in his hand causing it to spill a little. Then he poured himself one as well.

It wasn't yet midday.

Ellie looped off her plastic backpack, its stiff material catching against her shirt. Granny shoved a serving tray beneath her nose.

Rows of sandwiches were cut neatly into squares and arranged in an orderly fashion. Chicken, lettuce and mayo. Ham and cheese.

Plus, the holy trinity—cheese and gherkin with the crusts cut off. She couldn't say no to cheese and gherkin with the crusts cut off.

'Hungry, darling?'

It was her death row meal served on a silver platter.

'Ellie darling, don't you want a sandwich?' her Granny's words were the noose. Ellie's mother's eyes the rifle. Her father chose ignorance as he talked to Grandpa's wig.

'No thanks, Granny,' Ellie swallowed. 'I—I made jewellery. Wanna see?'

'Later, deary.' Granny's said as she glided away. 'What's wrong with her, Julie? She'll usually eat anything.'

Julie smiled blandly at her mother-in-law.

Not her real smile, Ellie knew. Not the one they shared while she watched her mother getting a pedicure. Nor the secret one father got for doing the washing-up. It wasn't even the smile she used on the salesman at K-mart to get a refund without her receipt.

Ellie fiddled with the zip on her backpack, desperate to get out her Polly Pocket doll.

Julie was a predator as she turned back to Granny. 'Hear what happened to the Barettys?'

Defying her age, Granny moved fast as an emu into the seat opposite. 'Is this why they weren't at lawn bowls?'

Mother gave a slow nod. Looked to be savouring the tasty morsel she held in her mouth. Rolled it around with a sip of wine. Granny didn't breathe. Her focus held the intensity of the laser show Ellie had seen on Australia Day. The lights beaming across the Swan River had seemed alien. Otherworldly.

'I thought you'd already know by now, Sybil.'

Father was glued to the TV. It was a replay of an old game from last season. Ellie hadn't known her dad even liked football. Was this his favourite team? She'd have to ask him later. Ash winked across the table, before diving behind the cover of a magazine. Her nose pressed so closely to its pages that its ink might smudge onto her face. Perhaps that could be the beauty trend she tried next. The ombre nails had been fun at least, better than the failed eyelash extensions. Ellie stifled her giggle amid the quiet. Grandpa sat motionless but his watery eyes held strong. She followed his gaze back to her mother.

Mother sighed and reluctantly said, 'It was a bad investment.'

'I told Lynette that I thought they'd gone broke. I told her that!' Granny exclaimed feverishly. 'Wait till the bridge girls hear about this.'

Julie shrugged, shoulder pads settling back against the wicker-framed seat. 'It's not a real surprise. Ted always was a loose cannon. She should've pulled him in once he'd sold their shares.'

'That's what you get for investing in,' Granny paused, before hissing through narrowed lips, '*foreign companies*.'

Ellie stopped listening, instead she stared longingly at the food. Why had nobody touched the food? Not even the mini quiches had gotten a look in by her dad. Ash never seemed hungry these days, too preoccupied. Saliva pooled in her mouth at the sliver of gherkin peeking out from the corner of one sandwich. The droop of its green body was a limp invitation. Ellie sat quickly on her hands.

Movement through the sprawl of the kitchen captured her attention. Grandpa opened the cutlery drawer and stood staring at its contents. He shut the drawer. Pulled the drawer out again. Grandpa's cardigan swung low as he bent to watch the drawer creaking along its wheels, face bent close to the forks. Back and forth. Open and shut. What look marked his face—scrutiny? Confusion?

'... isn't that right?' Mother looked at her expectantly.

She hadn't been listening.

'Huh?' Ellie regretted her response immediately.

She received a foreboding look. '*I was saying* how beautifully you performed in the flute duet for the performing arts festival.'

Beautiful? Even Ellie knew *passable* was a stretch. A last-minute call-up, she'd been lucky to keep up with the supporting harmonies to Castle on a Cloud. She certainly wasn't given the honour of leading melody like Janine Jurnte.

But she nodded. 'Yes, we um, we got a commendation.'

Janine got the commendation. Mr Bell called her a prodigy. If Janine's playing was an expensive box of Cadbury chocolates, Ellie's was the home brand kind parents put in lolly bags. Stale, chewy and generally best avoided if you didn't want a broken tooth.

'That's lovely, darling. I would've thought guitar or piano would be more useful though,' Granny murmured, musing as she sipped her drink. 'Isn't flute usually one that the Asians play, Julie?'

Mother's answering cough was loud and spluttering.

'I would've thought it best left to them. But I could be wrong.' Granny spun the lazy Susan in the centre of the table.

The mini quiches danced past Ellie in a blur.

She forced her mind to wander off and look away from the food. The conversation was so much of the same. Besides, Polly Pocket sought adventure. Maybe they'd land in New York or swim off a deserted island. Straightening the doll's tiny legs, she explored the red dirt of Kalgoorlie.

Ash had laughed at Polly a few months ago. Glancing at her mates, she'd said, 'It's a bit juvenile.'

The barb still stung. Even if she was right. Her friends had cackled as they moved to the back lawn, stripped to their swimmers, and coated their bodies in cooking oil. Another hot tip Ash had read about in her mags. They looked ridiculous, like the slimy sausages her father cooked on the barbeque. Ellie kept herself scarce when they were around. Ash was different in front of her friends. No singing, not like they did in the car. No games. No swinging on the Hills Hoist. Instead, she and her friends talked about something called a vibrator. It sounded like a low-budget horror film.

So, Ellie and Polly Pocket played by themselves. It was better in secret anyway.

The clunk of his cane marked Grandpa's approach. He seemed to move through a room like he never quite knew she was there. Maybe he needed glasses rather than a new wig.

'Polly's off adventuring.' She gestured to her doll, its plastic body coated in an orange dress.

Grey, unfocused eyes watched her. Her grandpa didn't speak much. He squeaked chalk onto an old pool cue. It was painstakingly slow, and the chalk missed the cue often. Ellie left Polly on the green felt and looked at the pictures on the side table she'd walked past a million times.

Granny was dressed in a sparkling ball dress, a long cigarette dangling from a gloved hand. Her dad as a kid on a bike at Rottnest Island. Grandpa in a beat-up ute surrounded by endless red dirt, long hair draped down to his shoulders.

'You had hair?!' She clapped both hands over her mouth.

Grandpa's lip twitched.

'Sorry Grandpa. I—uh—that was rude.' She hurriedly turned her attention back to the photos.

But Grandpa was staring at his pool cue.

More pictures lined the side table, each coated with a fine layer of dust. Her father and her grandparents at a school award ceremony, her dad's shoes impossibly polished. Granny with her bridge group, their faces severe and stiff. One picture was tucked in tightly behind and Ellie tugged it forward.

A young Grandpa smiled broadly at the camera; his arms clapped around another man's shoulders. Their uniforms were neat, although Grandpa's shirt gaped open at the collar where a silver necklace hung loosely. A gun was slung casually across the other man's shoulder.

Again, that full hair stood proudly on his head.

She chewed her lip and asked softly, 'How old are you there?'

He glanced at the picture she held out. He took it, his gaze lasting for endless minutes. She longed to bounce on each foot, to shake off the energy bubbling within her body. Polly begged her from the pool table to run toward another adventure. But Grandpa's stare was the distant sun—usually cloudy eyes shining clear.

Ellie thought about the guns, the uniforms. This was his time at war. 'Were you scared?'

The wig considered her, several hairs pointing north on their own journey. He answered with a nod.

Grandpa dipped his chin a second time, indicating a pair of leather armchairs in the corner. Ellie sat heavily, tugged at the place where her shirt touched her belly. A button had popped off that morning when she'd gotten dressed. She tried to curl up in the seat like her mother always did but ended up getting one leg awkwardly stuck.

Before Grandpa joined her, he reached under the cupboard of photographs to a devious door embedded in the framework. Its handle was a subtle curve she hadn't realised was there.

He fumbled around inside, eventually pulling out a metal tin. Grandpa sat down with the creak of his knees. His solemn face was grave and eyes focused. Charged with a purpose she didn't quite understand as he held it out to her.

An unremarkable thing. The sort of lunchbox kids would get teased at school for owning.

She fingered the edges of it. Scratches marred its colour. Sunlight glinted on the etching on its side. A wing? A tail? It'd almost faded beyond recognition.

'Gecko,' she read the word written in small gold lettering.

Grandpa's thumb rubbed back and forth a few times over the image of his uniformed buddy. A snapshot of another life.

'That's Gecko?'

His answering smile was small. But colour returned to his cheeks. Grandpa took the tin back from her, its contents rattling. Shaky hands took several tries to crack the lid. Its screech was as angry as Granny on Christmas Day. Always determined to have a ham sandwich under the tree alone.

Conspiratorially he held a finger to his lips. A secret just for them. The pang of her mother's disapproval was forgotten. Ellie surged forward to look inside.

Anzac biscuits coated the bottom of the lunch box. A smattering of broken bits littered around as Grandpa lightly shook the tin.

Biscuits were her favourite. Behind gherkin and cheese sandwiches with the crusts cut off, of course.

Ellie smashed one into her mouth. 'Fhhnanks.'

Grandpa's answering grin was crumb-covered. He gently flicked them off with hairless hands and leant the tin toward her. Her thick hands snatched another biscuit. A closer inspection revealed the oats were crispy, the edges golden.

The chair creaked as she leant towards him. 'Did you bake these?'

But she'd lost him to the dusty picture. Gaze adrift in the embrace of a young man once called Gecko. The wig watched from its perch, peering down at the golden locks that'd covered Grandpa's head. Could wigs feel jealousy? His old hair wasn't so different from the lengthy bob permanently stuck to Polly's head.

'Your mother wants to leave.' Granny's voice slithered down the hallway.

His eyes snapped up to hers. Tin lid clanging shut; they hid the evidence. Their brief hug was the toy found at the bottom of a cereal box. Unexpected joy.

'Ellie? *Quick, quick.*'

Granny strode to the front door, the silver platter still looming on the dining table. Sandwiches with arms outstretched. But Ellie didn't even glance at them.

'You can show me the jewellery next time.' Granny patted her on the back.

Grandpa made the slow descent down the driveway as she padded ahead to the car.

'Hurry up, Ellie—we have to get Ash to a BBQ at the Clarences' place.' Her mother shut the passenger door.

Ellie climbed in. Grandpa's secret tucked deeply in the seams of her pockets, alongside Polly. The sigh from her father was audible as the engine rolled over.

'That's the box ticked for another week.' Her mother threw a genuine smile at her in the backseat.

She caught it with both hands.

Ellie waved vigorously to Grandpa as they drove away. He saluted with his cane, his wig winking in approval.

Reborn as Rekha

Ashley Somwaru

Bleach. That's what I thought of when I looked in the mirror today. The amount of Fair & Lovely lotion I rubbed into the corners of my mouth so that the purplish-brown spots would disappear, so my lips would look more kissable. The spots are back. Maybe they never went away.

Stuck in past memories, I'm wearing a white sari. My face matches the dupatta pinned to the parietal area of my head. Part of me is still spinning in a crowded room even though I am now sitting motionless in a wooden chair listening to a child cry for French fries. *When you go home you can have it*, the mother whispers, her back turned towards me. The child plants himself on the floor and bawls. Then the mother is on the floor, coaxing her child. I think to myself: Is this what I'm missing?

If I look at my hands, they are still a dark henna red, the blood of my father's birth rights. I walk around without a last name. I tell people I don't know what an elephant's cry sounds like, but I know its silence. I know the pain of breaking my body in the name of ivory in a quest to enchant you. I offer salaam before I draw the dupatta over my eyes.

I don't want to get up from the spot I made for myself on the floor when I started this dance—in Seiza position—only the beat increases. When I close my eyes, I feel Nataraja's feet are my feet, his hips are my hips. I am dancing for myself, on this stage I've created. I don't care for the eyes turned towards me.

In Ankhon Ki Masti Ke, I can tell you all my stories, but slant. I will no longer speak the language I was born with but the language you want to hear, if that makes you more willing to listen. You'll have to pay attention carefully as the *ghungroos* around my feet get louder and louder. No, I won't stop clicking my toes and heels to the ground. My head will continue ticking, counting the syllables. My fingers will rip the clouds from the sky. My voice will echo—you may get vertigo.

I have always loved running through rose gardens—the leaves against my pudgy arms—I never felt the thorns. I have always loved my hair braided until my mother no longer threaded the ends. Then, I was all lion mane but no roar.

Somewhere, in a past memory, I watch a woman named Taramatie sing Dil Cheez Kya Hai to her niece who asks her if she is Rekha. She says 'yes' because she's never held onto a man long enough.

Truth is, I want to be all women. I want to be Mansi, head tilted back in a moan of pleasure. I want to be Aarti—rising from the water—putting a knife to my husband's throat after he pushes me off a cliff. I want to be Jyothi, the body that rises out of the water after the crocodiles finish feasting on my thighs. I want to be Chandni, the heartbroken. Umrao, the courtesan. Sarita, the ghost. Bhanurekha, the sunrays. Rekha, the lines I draw across your forehead.

Please don't ask me about love letters and ceiling fans. I don't want to remember my love, hanging from the blades. I no longer want to write love letters. I no longer want to think about how they will hang my body right next to my love, who is still airborne.

Silsila in Hindi means a continuation. In Arabic, it means a chain. I am locked into a vision you wish to see of me—a woman killing her husband, a woman chasing after another woman's husband, a woman hungry for men. I have breaking news for you. I don't eat the flesh of men, no matter how tempting.

I paint my lips maroon. I wrap my hair in jasmine, layer my cheeks with *paan* leaves, tie my wrists with bells. Like this, I climb to the highest point of the Catskill Mountains to greet the sunset. Like this, I sing to the Eiffel Tower with the cheapest bottle of champagne in hand. I catch a bus to Brussels, stroll through the flower carpet festival, the scent hanging in my hair. Like this, I walk through farming fields in Cuba, picking crown flowers, grinding mint next to lettuce to capture the flies. Like this, I walk through a *rudraksha* tree forest in Kauai, stepping on my prayers, crunching them under my feet like leaves. I slip into the white sands of Turks and Caicos and watch the waves sing the blue sky to sleep. I search the streets of Copenhagen until I find a colourful line of houses like those seen in postcards. I drive to a dried waterfall in Guatemala. Like this, I have seen the world but never regained my love.

In disappearance the mind resets. People no longer remember me as the killer of men but as a singer of stories.

The wrinkles in the corners of my mouth are as much from laughing as sobbing. I sing nursery rhymes to the child I'll never have so she can sleep soundly. I pat my back until my eyes droop and everything is yellow-hazed like sunrise. I kiss the cheek of my niece and tell her, even if you can't hold onto a man, hold onto yourself.

I put on my *ghungroos* and spin. Let your eyes be the jewelled *bindiya*. Let your eyes adorn. I gift my heaving shoulders gold silk, my quivering lips an unstrung veena, turning my voice into what their fingers will pluck.

If you happen to see me again, wandering through the fruit markets in Skeldon or sandboarding in Chile, point me in the direction of home. Tell me the rewritten version of me is welcome.

Remember me tapping Jag Ghoomeya over my heart.

Like this, remember me, reborn, spinning until the music stills.

The True Light of Day is Constant

Catherine Armitage

If the light behind your eyes is pulsing, the machines you're hooked up to are winning and it's night. The true light of day is constant. A few times you happen to be awake at the start. You hear the first footsteps then the whirr and snap of blinds on their rollers, then slowly, slowly, the light suffuses behind your eyelids and the pulses fade. In time there will be more footsteps and lowered voices will drift around you, unfathomable. You lie still, as if you are in a coma, which you might be.

And later, days or weeks or months, your eyes open and your mother is sitting beside you—perhaps she has been there all along. She leans forward and wets your face with her tears.

She tells you not to talk, that you've cracked your skull, something to do with the horse and she's sorry she let it all happen.

You try to say something necessary, something unspeakable, but it's stuck among the cottony stuff that fills your mouth. It has to come out, this urgent, foul thing.

'Tampon.'

Your mother blinks, her eyes full of questions. 'Tampon?'

You attempt to nod, but your head doesn't seem to move, so you try the word again. This time she gets it and she's up and gone. You hear muffled voices and rapid footsteps. At the zing of the curtain rings on the rail above you, the light changes and someone is fumbling between your legs, and you feel a tug and then there's the smell.

'Didn't think to look down there. We were focused higher up,' someone says. It must be a nurse.

Sharp words shoot around you. You struggle to tune in over the static. Can that sharpshooter be your mother—your gentle, reticent, frightened mother?

You want to ask if your 'father' will come, your shouty, angry father, and then you don't. It's easier to stay asleep. But your mother tells you anyway. She says he wants to come, but he's taking your accident hard.

Exhaustion engulfs you. You wake to the clip-clop of hooves on lino. All the patients sit up in their beds and the nurses line up to watch your father make his way along the ward. Someone runs out to find a chair for him and comes back dragging it across the floor. His horse legs stick out from it at ridiculous angles. You can tell he's annoyed.

'I am not your father anymore,' he says. 'I am Lightning.'

You wait. This new trick of his is leading somewhere.

'It's time to get up,' he says. 'We're going for a little walk. Somewhere secret. Somewhere nice.'

'Does the shed need cleaning?' you ask. It's a little joke between you. That was his old trick, to get you in there.

He laughs. 'No, nothing like that. You'll see.'

You float beside him down the ward, your useless trailing legs next to his clip-clopping ones, past twenty pairs of astonished eyes on stalks. Some of the eyes break away from their moorings to join your procession down the stairs. You glide out the front door of the hospital and along a glowing path to a willow glade where a glistening pond beckons.

Your uncle—'father', 'Lightning'—stands at the edge, ears erect, thin long head nodding. 'Go ahead,' he says.

You can feel the goggling eyes bobbing at your back as the silken water tries to pull you in.

Sport rattled the rickety door and peered into the windowless tack shed, beyond the reach of the farm's electricity. When the rapid shadows of rats were gone from the rafters she stepped into the gloom. Once, opening the door to get the rifle—back when her real father was teaching her and her mother to shoot 'in case someone comes when I'm not here'—she had dislodged a sleeping possum.

She could have pulled the saddle from its stand and the bridle from its nail with her eyes shut, she'd done it so often. Yet she knocked her uncle/father's old Akubra off its hook beside the rifle rack.

He hated anyone to touch his hats, even those he'd retired to the shed. She dropped the saddle to retrieve the hat from the cement floor and pinched its crown back into shape with her fingers.

She is a growing girl on a white pony named Thunder and she's just won her first ribbon at a gymkhana. She is cantering from the show ring towards her new father who used to be her uncle, anticipating his praise. As she approaches a sudden gust plucks the hat from his head and drops it on the ground between them. Because Sport cannot stop her in time, Thunder tramples it. A few people see it happen and laugh. Sport knows her new father will be furious and weeps with silent fear.

He says nothing but pulls the car and trailer over to the side of the road on the way home. Then he says, 'Get out,' and reaches for the riding whip. He says, 'If you tell your mother, I'll flog you again. No one is interested in your tears.'

'C'mon, Lightning, c'mon,' she shouted in her deepest voice. It was embarrassing, but it was how everyone called their horses, and there was no one around to hear. From the furthest corner of the paddock, on the other side of the creek, Lightning twitched his ears but kept his head deep in the grass.

Thunder and Lightning were her new father's choice of names. He liked to say he had naming rights because he paid the bills. 'Another mouth to feed,' he said when Lightning arrived. 'It's a good thing I don't go around sowing wild oats like some men in this town.' This was him in a jokey mood at the breakfast table one morning, punching her mother's arm. 'I prefer to sow my oats at home.'

It took her years to realise what this meant. Longer still to comprehend the bitter harvest.

He tolerated her real name, Willow, at first, when her real father was freshly dead. Back then her new father still saw a football team of sons in his future. But when the sons didn't come, in that time when her mother got smaller and stayed inside, he started calling her 'Sport' instead of Willow and so did everyone else.

She walked back into the dark shed and dipped a bucket into a barrel of feed. Outside she shouted again, swivelling the bucket by the handle so the grains swished loudly. The horse broke into a loping trot, heading towards her through the creek where the water splashed silver on his belly in the sun. She watched to see if he was still limping from the previous weekend.

Some people loved their horses. Sport wanted to. She loved the feeling of communion between horse and rider when their bodies moved in synch, the pulsating rhythm of a fast canter, the surge of power before a jump. But two weeks after the hat incident with Thunder, she'd come outside to find the little mare gone and the big black gelding, Lightning, in the paddock instead. 'Today's pet is tomorrow's pet food' was another thing her new father liked to say. She had to find something hard in herself to stop the tears from coming, to block out the thought of her doomed pony in the knackery yard, quivering with fear as a stranger shot a bolt into her brain. She learned that the only safe way to be attached to a horse was firmly in the saddle, and even that wasn't safe.

Lightning had disliked being handled from the start. He would lash at her with his hooves if she were within striking distance. If her new father saw, he would grin and say that the horse still had a bit of stallion in him. But she read an article in a horse magazine that said snappishness and aggression could be a sign of past trauma in a horse, same as in a person.

A 'quiet yet formidable resistance' was another sign of maltreatment. The weekend before, Lightning had baulked at three jumps in a final's competition, just when they were showing him off to prospective buyers. The judge's elimination bell rang in her head as she and Lightning walked from the arena with the town's gaze on them from the grandstand, where her uncle/father sat with a person who had offered a big price. The force field of her uncle/father's anger enveloped her even from that distance.

When she got back to the mounting yard, he pulled her from the saddle and mounted Lightning himself. With rage-clenched teeth, he whipped the horse around the yard until it was limping with exhaustion. A pall of disapproval followed them back to their rig. As usual nothing was said on the way home, but after Sport went to bed, she heard him shouting in the living room.

That night in her bedroom as she fell asleep, she wondered how she would look back on it all, from a distance. Soon she'd be off to the city, to university. Her great escape, her uncle/father called it.

Lightning let her slip the bridle over his ears and the bit into his mouth when he came up for breath from the bucket. She tied the reins up short to the railing to prevent him from swinging his head around to bite her while she saddled him.

All above was dark with wings. A single black cockatoo separated from the roiling mass and swooped down to where she lay. Its raucous cry—'not yet, not yet'—was taken up across the sky. With its beak the bird plucked a brown hair from her head and carried it back to the cloud above. Another bird followed it and another and another, on and on.

She looked down and saw that her boots had dissolved into the dirt. Where her feet should have been, her legs tapered into slender points that pleased her but had nothing to do with the ground.

Lightning stood at the fence. With an immense effort, she rose to meet him. As she came closer, he let out a shrill whinny of alarm that lodged in her head at its highest pitch. When she reached out to touch his shoulder, he reared up on his hind legs and pawed at her.

She felt lighter as she floated up the ramp to the back door of the house. She understood that she should not try to open it but should pass through it, as an act of will. She sensed its resistance as she propelled herself to where the telephone sat on its table in an alcove off the kitchen.

She placed her arms carefully along the chair rests and sat. Her head fell forward. A great wet sound filled her head, urgent and angry like water rushing over a dam wall. She tried to shut it out, tried to think.

The telephone. She pulled her head slowly upwards and opened her eyes. She lifted the receiver, put it to the tumult in her ear and dialled a number. She said her name, and then, 'Something's gone wrong.' She thought there might be other words, but none came to her. Her voice sounded strange, like it belonged to someone else.

After a while she noticed the rushing noise had stopped. There was only the feeling of ebb and flow, gentle surge, soft retreat. She felt her limbs relinquish their angles as she rose from the chair and looked down at her slumped body.

Shadow and light played in the distance before her and the vast depth below. A female figure drifted out of the dark, mouthing her name, like a kiss. She became aware of others all around, drifting aimlessly through the rooms, her name on their lips. It was a welcome. She was one of them.

Her hands were gone, she noticed.

The true light of day is constant. It's there in your bedroom at home, a radiant frame around the window blind. Then you remember the crack of the rifle shot that woke you.

You slow-motion-scramble out of bed. You feel the cold floorboards at your feet and the soft belt of your dressing gown in your hands. Your extremities are sending signals to your brain again, as the doctors promised they would. At the back door, you pull on gumboots and clump down the ramp in a plodding rush.

Around the corner past the tack shed, you see the rifle leaning against the railing next to your mother.

She turns at the sound of your coming. 'I'm sorry darling. It had to be done.'

Down the paddock, you see your uncle on the ground by the creek, next to Lightning.

'It was the kindest thing to do,' your mother says.

Overhead, a black cockatoo wails. Your uncle sees you and gets to his feet. He is wringing his hat in his hands and weeping as he walks towards you.

The hard thing he made in you speaks.

'Tomorrow's pet food, huh?'

Your mother says, 'Your uncle is to blame. It's his shame.'

Not your 'father' anymore. You hear, for the first time: the hard thing your uncle made in you, it's in your mother too.

Sobs erupt like lava from your uncle. One of them is a word.

'Sport.'

'It's Willow,' you say. 'My name is Willow.'

Your mother takes your arm and together, you turn back for the house. Your uncle picks up the rifle.

How do you Lose a Whole Person?

Katy Knighton

We were together for the last time.

You'd invited me for lunch at The Journal café, but I don't remember eating. Before you'd even finished your coffee, you wanted me to come outside while you smoked. You needed a cigarette but maybe something else was making you jumpy. My baby moved inside me, and I glanced longingly at the display crammed with tortes, croissants, and gateaux.

Flinders Lane had a gusty loneliness. I tried not to breathe your second-hand smoke into my unborn child, who wrestled away from a particularly frigid blast of winter air to an uncomfortable spot under my ribs. The lower corner next to Degraves Street had street art saying HELP PLEASE GOOD WITCH at the height someone would squat to beg. You motioned to the writing. No one seemed to notice it except us. I wondered whose begging spot it had been, and how long since they had vanished forever.

You told me your short-term memory had gone due to the treatments in various hospitals dotted around Melbourne. Instead of an architecture career, you had a volunteer position at an op shop. You had a tiny flat, your tropical fish had died, and you struggled to keep a routine. It was so far from your teenage fantasies.

You struggled with your cigarette stub, turning from the wind.

We were both bloated, you from antidepressants, me from being eight months pregnant. I had meant to ask you to be godmother to my unborn child but thought I'd ask you next time I saw you, not realising this was our final meeting.

People streamed around us. Ten years ago, as schoolgirls, we would covertly gather details to discuss on our train ride home. We collected city personalities, using them to fabricate stories.

That woman with the white hair runs a lab called The Happiness Factor. Ironically, she's miserable.

The old man wearing a bowler hat steals art from corporate foyers; he's on his way to the Cadbury Building.

We made eye contact with each other when a good one for our old mental catalogue went past. That hadn't changed.

The CAE building caught my eye. I'd studied photography there, and you'd done various classes.

'Do you remember doing belly dancing?'

'Oh, yeah!' You sucked in some smoke to disguise not recalling.

'I heard the top floor of the Manchester Unity is for sale.' You'd always loved that building, with its fairytale quality.

'How much?'

'I don't know. Millions, probably. Do you want to go for an inspection?' I joked.

'Now? I don't know.'

The street art caught my eye again, reminding me.

'Hey, *The Wizard of Oz* is showing at ACMI this Saturday. Are you free?'

'Umm.' You struggled to process what I was asking. 'What? Oh. I don't know.' Your eyes searched for an answer in the sky.

'We could look for baby stuff afterwards.'

That was when you stubbed out your cigarette.

You asked if I could pay, and smoked another cigarette in a bitter gale, watching me from outside as I dealt with the bill. When I tried to hug you goodbye, you shuffled nervously as though static would spark between us and jolt you. After that day you disappeared. In your alternate life you would have walked to your architecture firm to birth new buildings, but instead the city swallowed you.

Our favourite part of Melbourne was the tiny staircase leading from Degraves Street to the Flinders Street Station underpass. From there, the tunnel opens out and leads, warren-like, to the train platforms. You and I imagined it could be anywhere we wanted, part of a foreign city, maybe even the internal organs of a film set. Within it were small shop fronts offering magazines, cheap books, postcards, socks, and chips. Everyone seemed impassive and busy. I theorised that they were androids populating the tunnels. You'd loved that idea.

We parted before the Degraves Street staircase. I lumbered painstakingly, trusting the steps that were invisible under my pregnant belly.

The androids kept moving at a steady pace and I wished you were with me so we could talk about them.

There goes a spy on her way to a meeting with an agent from Indonesia. He's reading a paper and she'll bump into him; that's how they exchange information.

Perhaps you'd followed me. I turned around to see. You weren't there.

I'm an idiot who lost her friend. The friend is gone now. I will miss that friend forever.

On the train home, I daydreamed until a filthy man plumped opposite me. I was reminded of other homeless people haunting the same locations every Saturday we'd visited Melbourne. We were convinced, in our game, that they were the only real people in the city.

Felt-head man, hair matted into a massive lump, ambles Swanston Walk. Distributes calm and order.

Singing lady warbling out of tune while holding an ice cream container, accompanied by rubbish bin drum man. They're always near Russell Street. Patron saints for getting rid of catchy pop songs.

You and I privately puzzled over their stories and gave them loose change that we'd saved up during the week. We said hello, shook hands.

Delta Dave.

I'd forgotten to tell you about Delta Dave.

I'd met his brother, who told me Delta Dave lived in a flat he'd bought with cash from busking. You would have been so happy to know that.

The stench from the guy opposite hit me. 'I'm Lucy. Have my ticket,' I said, offering it to him. I could always buy another.

'Nah. Nah ... they never fine me. Ha!'

His eyes slid over my huge belly. I could see him calculating what he could grift.

'Got money, though? Two dollars?'

I shook my head.

'Yeah, no one carries cash these days. Where've you been?'

I told him about lunch with my friend and all about how she'd been adopted, and never recovered from the abandonment of her birth parents telling her they didn't want to keep in contact.

'Must have been hard for her then, eh? Her friend, pregnant?

I stared at him. His grubby face examined me. *Where is my brain?*

It must have been so confronting for you—my giant belly full of a child who'd be my own, forever. In the excitement of seeing you again, I hadn't thought how it would affect you. Tears came.

The homeless guy put his filthy hand over mine.

'My stop,' I apologised, as I heaved myself up. 'Do you think ...' I started, but he interrupted.

'You're a good friend,' he replied. 'I can tell. Don't worry.'

Hannah and I had met when her family moved onto our hilly street. She was my age and would be going to the same High School. Our parents decided we should meet and clanged us together like cymbals one January afternoon.

Meeting her was awkward. I'm sure she felt the same way about me. That first day we couldn't find anything to say to each other and we didn't get along. My mum made it clear to me she was bitterly disappointed. At that stage she'd approved of Hannah and her parents.

It was only after our parents finally gave up trying that Hannah and I started hanging out. After school, the bus would drop us at the top of our street. We'd sit on the playground swings, look at the city skyline and dream of the future. The buildings were jagged teeth, the Rialto being the tallest. There were so many cranes. Sometimes, if the wind was just right, we could hear them working.

'I'm going to live there, one day, right in the heart. Will we be there together, do you think?' Hannah had asked.

I didn't know where the heart of the city was supposed to be. Instead of answering, I talked about being a child in the back seat of our family car, being driven home at night, winding up the steep ascent to Mount Dandenong. Melbourne had been a tiny metropolis, with fairy lights leading to the centre. Lots of people must live there. My mind couldn't fathom all the stories that those people must hold.

Hannah told me it sounded like I was looking at the Emerald City. It really felt like that.

As time went on we became inseparable.

I helped Hannah make models of famous buildings for practice, for the day when she'd be an architecture student at RMIT.

Hannah did impressions of all the teachers, in the change room after sport. For me. To make me laugh. At Assembly one time she went up to the microphone when the Principal was running late and did an impression of him. I told the school it had been a bet, and it was my fault. We had been suspended for a week and grounded for a month, but it had been worth it.

My parents told me that Hannah was a bad influence, but I told them to get stuffed. They had been aghast but powerless. It had been their idea to start with. Having Hannah as a friend felt like a superpower, giving me immunity against everybody at school who looked down on us.

It had been magical right until the end of Year Twelve. After High School I moved out of home as soon as I could, acutely aware of my parents' imminent separation.

You moved out, too. I'd assumed nothing would change between us. After a while you made excuses not to catch up. I was confused and hurt but I knew you were preoccupied, in the middle of plans to meet your birth parents.

It turned out that a few years after they gave you up for adoption, they got married to each other. They'd only been sixteen when you were born. You even had a full sister. Your birth parents wanted to see how you turned out; but when they'd seen, they turned their backs on you. They were perfectly happy without you. Maybe they were also deeply ashamed. It was a school day and your sister hadn't been there. You asked them if she knew about you. They said 'no'.

Then there were two suicide attempts.

I tried visiting after the first one, but I was told at the front desk that you weren't up to having visitors. The second time you were in a special clinic, all lemony-disinfectant, with tense staff and a glass air-lock style security door. I got permission to take you outside and we drove off.

What I'd really wanted was for you to say, 'Let's keep driving all night, and see where we end up.' The world whizzed by too fast. You made me drive back to the clinic.

After you were discharged, I visited you at home in your old bedroom. Your new best friend from hospital was there with you, laughing and taking up all your time.

I'd wanted to tell you about the architecture students with whom I shared my studio space and darkroom. They'd built mezzanine workspaces in the warehouse they'd leased, leaving the area underneath as a giant living room. They held outrageous parties and film nights. You would have loved those people, they should have been your people, and it should have been *you* introducing me to *them*.

One of them, Chloe, got me to come with her on a scouting mission. She led the way, scaling up the outside of the old Queen Vic Hospital using a rusty access ladder. My hands got sweaty and I freaked out but eventually made it to the rooftop.

We could see right across Melbourne.

Chloe pointed out the different heights of the buildings, the mish-mash of styles and the new architecture movement, façadism, designed to protect the fronts of old buildings so a new one could be put behind them. I took photos of the panorama for an assignment.

Deep inside the old Queen Vic the bottom two floors were dark and dripping. Chloe turned on her torch and held a finger to her lips. We heard other people moving around, talking about the building, their footsteps and voices echoing. Their noises were like a whispering heartbeat in the middle of the city. I swear I could feel ghosts. Being in that old building was like visiting a dying grandmother—it had wound down at the end of a long life of helping people. Six months later it nearly got demolished until it was discovered that ordinary women had donated money to have it built. When Chloe told me this anecdote I saved it for you.

I ran this story in my head while you giggled at an in-joke with your new friend, ignoring me.

I left and waited for your call.

Five years later you finally rang to invite me to The Journal for lunch. Getting this invitation was such a relief, but when we met up it frightened me how different your eyes were. Electric shock therapy had robbed you, emptied you. All the treatment, all the therapy and anti-depressants didn't seem to have worked. I didn't know what to do to help.

I made it worse.

Where were you? I'd tried calling but there'd been no answer. Soon after, my daughter took up all my time. I had Dorothy, who swept me up in her hurricane.

I drove to visit my parents, still living on the same street. Now Eureka was the biggest jagged tooth on the skyline.

'Are Hannah's parents still down the road?'

'No, they moved years ago,' said Mum as she plumped lunch in front of me. 'Have some extra.' She changed the topic, taking over feeding Dorothy who sat between us in her highchair. 'Coo, coo, little one,' she said, spooning food into her grandchild.

Dorothy said, 'Horse with blue head,' and even though I was driving I had to look.

The horse *did* have a blue head, covered in a flyveil. It reminded me of the albino horse we'd both liked at school camp in Year Nine. You helped put on his flyveil one time. It wasn't easy. We laughed like anything.

After I saw the blue-headed horse I tried calling you again, but someone else answered and told me it was the wrong number.

I drove to the little flat you'd told me about at The Journal.

Dorothy asked, 'What is this place?'

The old guy next door said that it was a halfway house. I asked him about you, but he said he'd given up noticing the halfway people. There was no hint you might still be there, but I left a note just in case.

My daughter hung on my arm and yanked. It was time to go.

'Mummy, why are we here?' she asked.

'I'm trying to find someone.' *I miss you,* I thought. It ached.

'If you wish hard enough, would she come back?' my daughter asked.

It was a gigantic problem. I missed you even more when she said that. *Why hadn't I tried harder?*

I saw you.

You had no shoes, your hair was all mad and unkempt, and you were going through the contents of a bin at Flinders Street station. My train pulled away. I had no way of letting you know I was there. I hugged Dorothy as the train gained speed, taking me away.

What killed me was that I knew your story. You weren't like the other down-and-out people. You were my Hannah. I didn't feel like a good friend. That homeless guy on the train had been wrong.

Dorothy and I visited my parent's house for dinner. I walked with my daughter up the hill to the playground afterwards. The old swing creaked as I pushed her into a daydream rhythm and thought of you. The crystal shards of Melbourne sparkled in the dying light like the Emerald City.

I knew where I was going to search.

Today I caught the train with my daughter. She fidgeted on my lap and licked her fingers, drawing slimy pictures on the windows. To distract her into behaving I told her about you and how we would make up stories about the city people.

'That man keeps a goat in his kitchen,' I whispered.

An old guy raised his gigantic hairy eyebrows at us. My daughter drew in her breath.

'Over there is a witch, a good witch who will cast a lucky spell on us if we smile.'

Dorothy twisted her head. The woman curled up her lips slightly when she saw my little girl grinning at her.

We dawdled among the pressing tide of people in the Flinders Street underpass. My daughter yanked my arm while I scanned faces, hoping to see you.

'She is hiding something in that bag, Mummy,' my daughter whispered, pointing.

I looked, hoping it was you. It wasn't.

'A packet of magic biscuits?'

'Yes! They each turn into kittens. If you eat them by mistake you die. Don't eat one, Mummy!'

I'd stopped walking. We'd reached the little staircase and you weren't there.

'What are we doing here, Mummy?'

'Looking for Hannah. I can't find her.'

'How do you lose a whole person?' she replied.

The Last Skywhale

Jacob Anthony Serena

We soared above the sand in those days. My sister and I perched on our harness atop the broad back of Benjin-cet. Endless dunes below, endless blue sky above, slowly sailing through it all.

Even now, the sharp ache of absence catches me at odd moments.

Rain would fall from Benjin-cet's great belly, the condensation collecting along his body in rivulets as we flew. His routes were obvious below, greentracks of growing life among the sand, flourishing in the precipitation of his many passings. We migrated above this wide tangled net of vegetation between the oasis settlements, trade routes from Mat Oasis to Jorg Oasis and all the way out to Bil Oasis. We even stopped at Paul Oasis to trade, although Medeev would make me wait atop the beached Benjin-cet while she trekked down to the market, her longblade sheathed but clearly visible on her hip. I would poke my tongue out at my sister's back as she left, but my hug when she returned was as strong as I could make it. I shouldn't have worried. Anyone with half a brain would trust a Pauler about as much as they would a scorpion—and believe me, this still holds true today—but even they needed the trade in Jorger building supplies or the spices from San Oasis we carried upon Benjin-cet.

Besides, Benji was gentle, but he was geologically big. And he knew who his riders were.

And then we'd be off again, to the next oasis, the next market, the next horizon.

Once I was old enough, Medeev would teach me what she knew about the skywhales as we flew. Things she had learned from our mother (who I barely remembered), things she had worked out for herself. The pod had once numbered in the dozens, rain showering down as they followed air currents and the clouds. Their steady migration formed the basis for the calendar we still used. She thought the clouds in some way contained their food source, as Benjin-cet would sometimes divert from his course for kilometres to find them, mouth gaping wide to strain cloud through curtains of baleen. His massive body would breach through the cloudbanks as he did this, and Medeev and I would hang on tight at the front of him, safely clipped but shrieking and laughing all the same, feeling the momentum of his motion deep in our bellies.

Benjin-cet was alone by then, as even skywhales must grow old and pass. But he still followed the air currents, still graced the dwindled greentracks below with his rain. The water, Medeev said, condensed along wide meadows of fur that she called his rainbelts as air filtered through them. She thought it might be a way to regulate his temperature or excrete excess moisture. Or maybe assessing the ambient humidity told him something about cloud movement. Or none of those. She wasn't sure.

She showed me other things. How to navigate by the sun and the stars. How to trade, as we practised haggling porridge bowls and cups of tea back and forth. How to maintain the kilometres-long chained bands of hardleather for the harness that secured our dwelling and trade storage to the sloping valley of Benjin-cet's back and the tracks of spaced-out carabiners we clipped our way along.

'We are not birds, we are not Benji,' Medeev would lecture. 'If we fall, we will not fly.'

I spent hours rubbing oils into the leather alongside Medeev, mirroring her smooth circles as best I could. My arms were sore when we crawled into our bed-bags at night, the gentle burn of a productive day.

She taught me how to care for him. At first, I thought she had me scrambling down cliff-like flanks to pry away puckerbugs and scrape moss from fin-folds just so she could have an hour or four of peace but, young though I was, I could hear the difference in his calls when I was done, the gratitude in them.

Don't get me wrong, it wasn't all lessons and work. Medeev was my teacher, but she was also, first and foremost, my sister. One day, somewhere out between the Niel and Petrandro Oases, she called me away from the endless leather polishing. 'It is time,' she said, holding my shoulder intently. 'You are ready for one of the great events of being a Rider.'

I was beyond excited. I was beyond nervous, too, though I would never show it. Not to brave Medeev.

We hiked most of a day down the corrugation of Benjin-cet's spine, steadily clipping our way beneath the great peaks of his primary and secondary dorsal fins to his tail. The carabiners here were dull from infrequent use, but sturdy still. The sun was descending behind us, and the glacial sway of his flukes left a serpentine contrail in his wake. I took all of this in with wide eyes while staring at Medeev, waiting for this event. She looked around as if assessing the area and apparently it satisfied whatever criteria she had in her head. She nodded, once, and turned that assessing gaze to me. I swallowed, stood straighter, the very epitome of a Skywhale Rider. Her eyes narrowed as she nodded again.

She had me sit facing Benjin-cet's tail, cross-legged, hands resting palms-up on my knees. She had me close my eyes, take deep breaths, in through my nose, out through my mouth. I was to reach out with all my senses and really *feel* Benji, Benjin-cet, every tectonic flex of his muscles punctuated by the fluttering ailron shifts of his countless tertiary fins. Hear the wind rustle through his rainbelts, feel it dance around my face, smell the scent of him it carried.

At peace, at one with Benji, I exhaled.

And took a deep breath back in, right as the skywhale farted.

We were seated somewhere above his drain, and everything about Benjin-cet was massive. This stench was no different.

Gagging, eyes streaming with tears, I wheeled around to see the traitor howling with laughter, mouth and nose safe behind the shelter of her raised flightveil. I made to yell at her but of course that only made it worse as I inhaled more of the gas, so truly rancid it made my head swim. Eventually, the air cleared, great Benjin-cet leaving behind his faint brown cloud, but the sporadic laughter of my beloved sister continued all the long way back to our dwelling.

It is a treasured memory. Almost as treasured as the one I have of, that same night as the traitor slept, slipping a puckerbug in among her bed-bag.

Eventually, too soon, all things end. Memories. Days and years. Even great Benjin-cet, last of the skywhales.

It is simply the way.

They dim quickly, Medeev would tell me later. That's what the records said, at least. I had not read them, but a deep part of me still understood what I was seeing. For an age, Benjin-cet had soared the sky, as mighty three centuries ago as he was in my youth. But the changes set in, over weeks and months. A year, maybe, all told. His fins seemed to stiffen. A new brittle paleness frosted the rainbelts and their rivulets slowed to trickles. He sang out less and seemed to go longer between chasing cloud banks. When we beached to trade at Legov or Surnai Oasis it felt like he flopped down upon the sands, rather than coming to rest on them, and he took longer to lift off again. I heard a Surnaier ask Medeev something with concern in his voice, but she brushed him off, her face impassive as stone. She was quiet as we polished the harness and at night we did not speak of it.

Once, I left without explanation for most of the day. Clipped along towards the front of him, down towards his eye. He saw me, sang out to me. I saw myself reflected in the long curve of his lens: a little girl, tear-strewn and smiling. Filled to bursting with a pre-emptive absence she couldn't fully understand yet.

Saw, too, the new cloudiness arcing all around the outer edge of his iris.

When I returned that night, Medeev didn't ask where I had gone. She just touched my shoulder and passed me dinner. That night we both slept in her bed-bag, warm and safe and together.

A week or so later, grief struck.

I don't think either of us was surprised. We were somewhere out past Kalyong Oasis, and Benji had veered away from the greentrack below as if on a cloud-chase. Only, there were no clouds. He swam out into clear blue. He sang out, once. And then, gently, gracefully, inevitably, he fell.

We cried, Medeev and I, as it happened and in the silence that followed his last landing. For days we did nothing, existed in a fog. The world made no sense. I would eat mechanically, and Medeev ate nothing at all if I did not hand-feed her. Finally, I shouted at her, shook her, and she came back from trying to follow him. To some degree, at least. I think a part of her, the deepest part, would always be listening for his song.

Time passes, and we go on. What else can we do? And even after his fall, Benjin-cet had one last gift for us. It took weeks but gradually his great body broke down. Swathes of skin and muscle changed, cracking and flaking away. Towering ribs became brittle, then crumbled into the dunes. Body and bone and sand mixed, became something else. This loamy ground seemed almost to want new life to grow from it, and grow it did. It flourished especially around the growing collection of water pooled above the remains of his furry rainbelts, first a boggy stretch, then a large pond, and finally an oasis proper. Benjin Oasis.

Once and always, Benji was our home, Medeev's and mine.

The world went on. Others made their way to the newest oasis once news of Benjin-cet's fall got out. Our family first, as was proper, but then others too. We used some of the trade goods Benjin-cet had been carrying to raise the first structures of our new settlement.

The rest were traded to re-establish contact and commerce with the other oases. Benjin Oasis became a natural hub, as Benjin-cet had fallen somewhere in the centre of the vast web of his old migration paths. I helped with this, using Medeev's many lessons well, striking out and retracing the circulatory pathways of our society. We lined them with new markers, the kite-poles. We maintain them still, small fabric whales tethered to wooden staves lining the desert, guiding us home. I would watch them as they bobbed and dipped in the breeze and think of cloud chases. Absence would choke me. And then recede to leave me smiling with bittersweet memory.

Slowly, pole by pole, we rejoined humanity. Benji was gone, and the greentracks withered away with him, but the Oasis People welcomed us back to trade and bicker and laugh and grow.

Medeev was never the same after Benjin-cet fell. Never quite came all the way back. She threw herself into life here, I know. Became chief, backed me in planning my many expeditions out into the sands, married Yesh and surrounded herself with children.

But she never travelled the sands again. Never left Benji. Most nights I would spy her sitting down by the banks of the oasis, trailing her fingers through his water or tilting her head up to his sky. Sometimes I would join her, shoulder to shoulder in silence. More often I would leave them be.

In turn, Medeev passed as well. That was ... hard, for me.

And so I am chief, guiding the day-to-day of Benjin Oasis. Younger, abler traders now trek the kite-ways, doing the oasis proud. My granddaughter, Deev, is among them, and I hang on to every word of the news and tall tales she brings home. I miss following the kites through the sands, of course, but my role and my life is here now. It is a good one.

It's quiet tonight, sitting in Medeev's place, down by the oasis banks. The water is quiet and glass-still, a perfect mirror for the full moon above.

The memories hurt, even as I hold them tighter. They wind through me, Benji and Medeev's many passings through my life, and I trek along them, along sights and scents and sounds bobbing and dipping before me in the breeze. I trek along them, and they're with me again. I trek along them, and I miss them, so much.

I will never come all the way back.

And that's okay.

The moon in the water is gently obscured by a passing cloud. I squint a little, tilt my head just right ... and smile through the salt of my tears. I am still smiling as I drift to sleep, drift away with the cloud that looks just like a great skywhale.

Endless dunes below, endless stars above, slowly sailing through it all.

The Jumps

Katherine Mann

Alana leads the way as we walk home from school. We follow the dirt road down the hill and into the cool air that drifts up from the creek. The creek bed is sand-lined, and we glimpse the silken black water as we cross the bridge. The trees crowd the sides of the road, tilting downhill to the deep ditch that cuts into the gravel edge. It hasn't rained for some time and the ditches are clustered with a glossy-leaved creeper, squirming in its dry bed. The treetops meet above our heads, forming a tunnel.

Dust clouds our feet. Bush flies circle Alana's white backpack. Several hitch a ride, land as black specks on her shoulders. She flails her arms around, slapping at herself. The insects lift, circle, land again. The dirt road meets tarmac ahead, the mouth of the tunnel opens to houses and cars, the factory built along the highway, bright light.

'Hurry up!' Alana doesn't bother to look back at me and Chris, trailing her like ducklings.

Three kids on bikes approach from behind, wheels whirring, gravel crunching and wild laughter. They swerve ahead of us, cut in front of Chris. 'Get outta the way, *freak*!' They stand on the pedals, swing the handlebars to speed up the hill. Their bodies cut long streaks, silhouetted by the bald sun. They all wear T-shirts that flap on gaunt chests. Arms of wire.

Chris keeps his head down and scuffs the gravel.

Dino, who is in the lead, stops when his tyres hit the tarmac, turns his BMX on the spot and laughs. His head is shaved, except for a bleached blonde fringe and rat's tail. Teeth like jellybeans. His figure is framed by the arc of trees, the sunlight glows around him and makes magic light of the dust rising from his trail.

'Fuck off, Dino,' Alana tells him.

'What are you standing up for that loser for?' Dino spits on the ground. The BMX skids, takes off, a blur of black and white checked padding, knobbly knees and spinning pedals.

'That bike is far too small for him,' I say.

'They've made some jumps in the paddock by Ben West's house. Want to go and check it out?'

I'm too surprised to answer her and instead look over at Chris to see what he thinks. I'm sure he's rolling his eyes, but I can't see because his face is turned to the ground.

We emerge into the sunshine, the bright light and heat hitting our faces from the west. I raise my hand to shield my face, squint and look around. The sealed road rises in the direction of Ben's place. The smell of cooking wheat, the hum of the factory. Matthew Dwyer, James Kent and rat-face Dino are doing lazy circuits of the tarmac where it spreads out at the slow bend. They take a car head-on, gracefully swerving into its slipstream as it passes, hard on the horn. Matthew looks over his shoulder, gives the driver the finger. 'Get it up ya, dickhead!' he hollers. They slip away, up the hill to a gutter lip that leads into the paddock alongside Ben's house.

Alana turns after them.

'It's shorter if we go that way.' I gesture downhill, towards the Catholic church, its slipshod timber sign on the edge of the footpath.

'I'm bored,' Alana answers.

She keeps walking past the seeding grass, the ditch cut into the bank. She moves onto the road, walks down the centre of the hot tarmac. A dog is going in the opposite direction. Whirring insects. A march fly's heavy buzz. The dog pricks its flopped-over ears, watches us pass, releasing a low, chest-thrumming growl.

'Piss off.' Alana scoops a stone, piffs it in the direction of the dog.

The dog barks, a bellow from inside a bucket. Tail up, swinging, bristled hair along its back. It takes a step, exposes pink gums to Alana.

Chris pulls back behind me.

'Shit.' She picks up a bigger stone. Looks at me. 'I can run faster than you.'

'Don't throw it.' I look around, no collar, no owner in sight.

A stone sails over my head, hits the dog on the ribs and it makes a noise like a punctured tire.

'Chris!' Shocked, I gape at him.

'Come *on*!' He sets off at a run, backpack thumping on his back as he scarpers up the road, the way the BMX riders went.

'Wait!' I hesitate. The dog has recoiled, is paused between attacking and running.

'*Go!*' Alana pelts after Chris, who is already over the gutter, legs cutting through the long grass into the paddock.

The dog starts barking, but it's backing off now, hackles raised on its thick white neck.

'Shuddup!' I aim for the vicious, deep voice my father would use. Fling an arm out. The dog's ears drop for a moment, and I set off after Alana and Chris, terrified of the feeling of teeth on my ankle.

I stop at the paddock, clutch at the straps of my bag, face burning, panting. A narrow path slices through knee-high grass. There is dust, tyre marks. The boys have been here in the wet and their tyres have gouged holes, which are dry and hard now, crisp-edged meteor craters. Bullet-shaped seed heads top the grass stalks. The whole paddock is uncut and ripples like water when touched by the breeze. It stretches beyond the row of houses and down to a gravel carpark in the distance. The local supermarket. If there are snakes, I'll lay a foot on one before I see it. To the right, up against a paling fence that bows and leans at crazy angles, are the jumps. There are paths, narrow troughs that lead over small hills, cut away valleys. James is paused at the entrance of the obstacle course, sees us and gives a hoot. Dino and Matthew look over too. Ben, older than the others, stands near them, hands on hips. His T-shirt is tight over a broad chest and fleshy shoulders. His dirt-brown hair is cut like a brush over the crown and flat and long over the back of his neck. The exposed skin of his upper arms is sunburned. Behind him is an open gate, leading into an overgrown garden. A goat on a chain is near him. It's rubbing its nose on a corrugated iron lean-to.

James is off, legs whirring, he gathers speed over the first hump. But, his front wheel is sloppy and clips the hard earth. His speed flips him, straight over the handlebars, and he crashes to the bottom. Screams.

'He's stacked it,' Dino announces unnecessarily.

We all watch, wait for him to get up. The boys recoil from James' crumpled form.

'Is he bleeding?' Hushed words. Matthew is craning, one foot still on a pedal.

'Go and check!' Ben barks the order.

The goat releases an almost human cry; one of its horns rubs on the fence. A sawing noise.

James starts wailing. He's tangled in his bike, with one of his legs underneath its metal bones. The wheel rims are bent out of shape. Matthew drops his BMX and scrambles to the side of the jump. 'You orright?' He takes a shoulder, opens the boy up. There is blood. Coming from a messed-up nose, a gouged forehead. Worse is the elbow. As Matthew half lifts James, we can see the swelling of displaced bone pushing through the skin.

'Oh my God.' Alana sounds as though she's going to be sick.

James' wail is like a siren. A wall of noise. We're all stuck, frozen, staring in horror. Matthew drops him and he collapses back onto the ground, injured arm tucked beneath him.

The goat starts bleating, over and over, it sounds like a frightened child. The animal head butts the iron lean-to, which shudders and clamours. Ben stands back and lets it, a satisfied expression on his face. He seems to be enjoying himself.

'Get your dad, Ben.' Matthew's voice is lost in the noise, it fades out as though it was never there.

Mr West's hand rests on the gate post as he surveys the scene. We gawp back at him. James stays face-down in the trough, his sobs muffled. The knee-high grass whispers around us as a light, cooling wind combs through it from east to west. My bare calves are seed-head whipped, beginning to itch. Chris is staring, mouth open for the flies to get in. Alana can't stop grinning.

Mr West heaves a sigh as he looks down at James curled on his side in the foetal position, still tangled in the bike wreckage. Matthew is standing next to him, completely useless. Looking about, here there and everywhere.

'My arm!' The wailing goes on and on.

The goat cuts in again with a loud bleat.

'Shut up.' Simon West drops his hand into the grass, finds the goat's chain and gives it a hard pull. 'Fucking animal.'

'He's hurt himself.' Matthew takes a step away from James, towards Dino who is teetering at the top of the track on his bike. His impatient twitch says he just wants James to clear the track.

Mr West runs a hand over the hair slicked to his head. His barrel chest strains his T-shirt—Carlton United Brewery is stretched out of shape across the front. Someone else has followed him out. Another man, of similar age. Thongs, skinny calves and stubby shorts, a cigarette burning between tar-stained fingertips. He looks familiar.

James is attempting to stand up and we all turn our attention to him and the left arm he's bracing.

The new man sucks air through his teeth.

There is a pause as we all watch James struggle.

Mr West shakes his head in a disappointed fashion. 'What do you reckon, Jim?' he asks his mate. 'Call an ambulance?'

Jim has an expert look, the decision maker. 'Nah.' He flicks his cigarette into the garden. 'It'll take too long. Gotta come from Jilton.' He looks us all over, scrutinising each face in turn. He pauses on me and Chris. He turns to Ben who is attempting to wipe the grin off his face. 'Those Theo Nightjar's kids?'

Ben gives a start, looks at us, shrugs.

Simon West starts towards James: his thongs slip under his feet; he stumbles and grabs at the fence post that is too far away. Simon's weight drags the chain, a sudden tug at the goat's neck. The goat, cropping at the long grass, is pulled off its feet. Simon goes down onto his hands and knees, half obscured by the grass. His sudden cry is high-pitched.

Ben snorts.

Jim's beating back a grin.

'What the *fuck* are you doing?' The words explode violently. Simon's face is livid, jaws working, spit on his lips.

Ben's face cuts blank.

Simon is stuck on one knee, struggling to get up. 'Get that animal inside before I shoot it.' His tone is vicious.

Ben jumps to obey and, in a shocked silence, he pulls the chain, drags the goat into the garden. We hear a gate clanging.

Jim appears taken aback at the outburst and looks in the direction of Ben's disappearance for a moment, before turning back to Ben's father. Coughs into his fist.

James gives a shuddering sob. He has rubbed the blood around his face and it is now smeared up into his hairline. He has abandoned his bike on the track and, cradling his left arm, begins to scramble towards the two men. Blood is dripping down the front of his T-shirt.

'Orright, Simon.' Jim takes Mr West's hand to help him up. We all watch the two men struggle to get the heavy-set man onto his feet again. Jim braces himself and hauls, his toes tensed like wires, gripping into his thongs. Finally, Mr West rises, stumbles, half falls into Jim, who staggers back. Mr West straightens, breathing hard.

Jim clears his throat and smooths his rumpled T-shirt over his hard ball-of-a-belly. He looks at Ben's father as though the rest of us aren't here, like he's waiting for something.

Mr West wipes his face on the back of a forearm, leans onto the fence he can now reach and turns a dark look on the rest of us crowding around.

Jim jangles his car keys. 'I'll drive him.'

Ben returns and Jim looks him up and down, turns to his father. He continues, 'Don't worry about it, Simon. I'll take the kid up to the hospital. Ben can collect the bike and park it in the garden.' He nods at Ben. 'Right, son.'

Ben keeps his head down, but nods.

'Right!' Loudly, decision made, Jim places a hand into the middle of James' back, steers him into the garden. 'Car's this way. Don't bleed on the upholstery though, eh?' Forced joviality.

After they go, there is a long silence. Simon West shakes the loose gate post. Stares down at his son, like the reason for all his anger is right there. He turns away, starts limping up to the house. 'Do as you're told.' The words are flung over his shoulder. The gate swings shut behind him.

I nudge Chris' foot. We should go.

Ben takes a few steps forward. He climbs the first jump. Spits on the ground. He looks down at the bike, blank-faced. He's staring down at James' bike, but his mind is somewhere else. The front wheel has been warped by the impact. The thick rear tyre tread is worn, the wheel spins.

'Get the bike, Nightjar.'

I jump like I've touched an electric fence.

Alana laughs.

He's not talking to me, though. Ben's eyes are red, as though he's been weeping. He advances upon Chris, scrubbing his mouth with the back of his hand.

Simon West is disappearing around the side of the house. He has somewhere better to be. He pushes through the tall fig tree pressed against the side of the house, maroon fruit-like clustered bruises pull branches low with their weight. The fig leaves are rustling, a closing door behind him. Ben is looking everywhere but where his father disappeared. He swallows; his cheeks are ruddy, like a rough wet rag has been scrubbed over them. Like the way Mum might clean the food off Chris' face when he was small, when he'd had a tantrum at the table, food everywhere. Maybe when Dad had just left in disgust at the chaos in the kitchen. Like it was all her fault.

Ben turns his red face to each of us, eyes small. He pauses at Chris and lifts and then settles his jaw again, in a copy of the move his father made.

'Hey, shit face.' He addresses Chris, who is looking up at him, mulishly, teeth clenched.

The two gaze at one another, hatefully. Chris at least a foot shorter, scrawny like he's made up from a bundle of sticks.

'You gonna have a cry?' he asks Ben.

A noise bursts from Dino, shocked that Chris would dare speak like that.

Ben makes a sudden move. 'I'm gunna *make* you get that bike, Nightjar.'

Sandpiper

Gillian Hagenus

Once the owners leave, the first thing I do in each house is wander through the rooms and let Sandpiper claim the spaces she wants for herself. She likes the dark spots, the cold shadows. If there is a basement or an attic, Sandpiper gets it. She also likes closets that lock.

There's no shortage of shadows in any house, no matter how open-plan the living room, or how full and hot the summer sun. I gravitate towards light motes like a bluetongue, but Sandpiper is never more than a few metres away, watching slit-eyed from the corners. The only place that I get to myself is the bed but, even then, Sandpiper likes to visit my dreams once I fall asleep, her wingbeats distant earthquakes that rumble through the bed frame.

This house isn't as opulent as some others. But all the houses in Walkerville are nice. This is different. Places like Springfield have expensive price tags but are sinking into the earth with age. Septic tanks burst and possums eat through the roofs. In Walkerville, there are some newer houses mixed in with the old, sun-soaked properties made for families and retirees with too much money. Not a graveyard shift hospital janitor and a savage sometimes-bird. Dad says, if you're born on seaweed beaches, you carry seaweed with you wherever you go, and I've yet to prove him wrong.

The Hilliers' master bedroom is ideal for afternoon sleep after a shift but not a great Sandpiper deterrent. It's on the wrong side of the house to get afternoon sunlight and languishes in gloom. I lay half-buried under the white down-filled quilt and hear her wingbeats approaching like distant sirens, swear I can feel wind by my head as the earthquake hits. I ride out the buffeting, my gaze fixed on a single lace eyelet of the quilt cover. Next door, children squeal over the hiss-tick of a lawn sprinkler as the wingbeats recede.

I won't get used to this bed before my time here is up. The memory foam is a new experience. It helps track my sleep so that if I wake to find the mattress hasn't caved in around me, I can assume I've been restless, limbs never still enough for my body to leave a mould. The quicksand afternoons, when my cheek is so sunken into the mattress and I have to peel my eye open like skin off a pear, those are the days I forget where I am. The mattress at the last house was so hard it used to echo the drum of my heartbeat back to me. This one absorbs it completely, like an un-memory of my aliveness.

I wake half sunken, vaguely aware that something has hit the iron fence with a clang, but it takes a while for me to sit up, to un-suction my body from its indent. Sandpiper sits all sharp angles in the armchair in the corner, filing her nails into beaks, taking up space. I scrub hands down my face and pull at the elastic sleep stuck in my cheeks, urging my body to awareness.

'Somebody's in the yard.' My voice cracks.

'Let him come,' Sandpiper says with a kick in the corner of her lips.

I startle at the sound of an ice cream truck melody that blares through the house. The doorbell. Sandpiper starts laughing.

I untwist my clothes and hurry down the stairs, grateful for the thick carpet that muffles my clumsy, sleep-licked footsteps. I press my face to the peephole. Through the fish-eye lens, I watch two children fidget on the stoop.

I take an embarrassingly long time with the locks, my arms weak as a newborn's as I heave open the door. The boys are clearly brothers, bare-chested in boardshorts, the light-grey concrete on the veranda darkening with the water that drips from their hems. The smaller brother breathes heavily, his mouth opening and closing at me; they only blink, waiting for me to say something.

'Yes?' I manage.

'Who are *you*?' the younger one blurts. 'You don't live here.'

'I'm a friend of the Hilliers,' I say, because you never tell the neighbours that you're house sitting alone. It's my number one rule. Sandpiper doesn't get it. I hear the *shink shink* of a knife sharpener in the kitchen. *Let him come.*

'Can we get our ball?' the older boy says. 'It went over the fence.'

'Wait here,' I say. 'I'll bring it for you.' I shut the door on them and take a deep breath. Sandpiper laughs as I come through the kitchen.

'They're *children*, Sandpiper. Please.'

The ball is one of those rubber kickballs, TV caricatures long faded from being left in the sun. It sits innocuous in the shadow of the mandarin tree and its foetal-green fruit. But Sandpiper loves shadow, so it's Sandpiper's ball now. I could ask, but she won't give it back. I go back to the boys dripping and shifting on the veranda.

'I can't find it, sorry.'

'It went over. By the mandarin tree,' says the older boy. 'Can't we just go look?'

We stare at each other for a while and I wait for his resolve to weaken, but he stands defiant. His brother shifts behind his arm.

'If the wet's the problem, we can go get a towel and come back.'

'No. Sorry.' I shut the door before my resolve can crumble. I pray they don't come back with their father.

The ball starts a steady slapping against the wall in the garage.

Sandpiper yells *D*.

Smack.

Sandpiper yells *O*.

Smack.

Sandpiper yells *N*.

Smack.

The ball stops and Sandpiper's voice echoes, a warning squark. 'You better hope I don't make it to Y. You won't like what I do to donkeys.'

When I get back to the house from my shift, it's not quite dawn. My dad is here, somewhere in the house. His deep voice reverberates through the walls. His pleas ride the shockwave of Sandpiper's wings, which rattle the fridge as she drives by, dragging Dad behind her, shirt collar clasped in one taloned hand, the brothers' kickball balanced on the other. I ignore them. I pull out fast-wilting spring onions, chicken breast, dig around in the Hilliers' condiment shelf to find a half-used bottle of hoisin sauce with an acceptably old expiry date. These are the types of things homeowners never miss because they don't remember they ever had them in the first place. It's the kind of life Sandpiper thinks her antics will get us: one so filled with things that belong to me they don't even matter anymore.

Sometimes I like to sit out in the yards or on the balconies, lean out the windows of all the different houses and imagine myself pressing grooves into them. Not grooves like the memory foam mattress that forget your shape as soon as you leave them, but real, permanent grooves. For a moment I see the painting that I would put on the wall and a subscription paper sitting in its thin plastic on the driveway. I can imagine inviting my father in. 'So this is my new place,' I would say. 'I'm not on seaweed beaches anymore, Dad.'

But then the gig ends, and I can't get another lined up fast enough so I have to go home. To seaweed beaches. And Sandpiper is more a bird there than she ever is otherwise and spends her time swooping around the house with her earthquake wings. The days are all rumblings and tidal waves, dumping dunes of brown seaweed.

I go to the pantry and open the door wide. Sandpiper turns around and puts a finger to her lips and gently shuts it again, locking herself in the gloom. The pleas turn to groans of pain as the pantry starts tremoring, glass jars clinking against each other and Sandpiper yells *D*.

Smack.

O

Smack.

I abandon the dinner things and go outside to lean against the deck railing in the dawn chill and whittle my elbows down into the wood.

Smack.

N.

Smack.

A bird chitters somewhere in the garden. *Willy Wagtail.* It's almost instinctive, to name them. *Passerine bird.*

Dad fancies himself a birdwatcher and is always walking along as though naming birds like that makes him smart and interesting, but really, he just knows all the birds that everyone knows. Fairywren. Piping Shrike. Noisy Miner. Sandpiper.

K.

Smack.

We stride across the beach, bare feet scrunching into piles of seaweed, twilight wind turning Dad's loose shirt into a parachute.

A racket in the bushes.

'Sandpiper, most likely.'

We walk.

'Seagull,' I say seriously, and point, 'a rare breed of bird.'

Dad doesn't say a word. So. Not a day for joking then. The beach is emptying quickly, the last of the warmth disappearing with the sun lying down on the water. The wind sets about making a nest of my hair and the seagull hops and flings an abandoned chip.

'I'm going to turn back,' I yell into the wind.

'Tell your mother I'll be at the pub.'

I won't need to.

Smack.

N.

Smack.

She'll make it to Y. She's got a point to prove today.

After Sandpiper has finished in the pantry and the house has settled into that new-house silence—not shifting and groaning on old-house bones but whirring faintly with appliance noise—I mull over getting back to dinner, or just leaving it and going to sleep. It's mid-morning on a Monday so there are no whipper snippers droning in the street and the neighbours' boys are likely at school, the house on the other side of the fence quiet for the first time in two days. I could get a good sleep. Sandpiper doesn't usually feel the need to earthquake my dreams after she's had a good kill, her appetite for savagery satiated, if only briefly. She knows, as I do, that we'll be back at Largs Bay by week's end. Sandpiper has no power in that house. So many shadows, but none of them hers.

In the end, my stomach wins out, so I untangle myself from the couch where I have been refreshing the Adelaide house sitter's site. I hesitate before the door of the pantry.

Sandpiper's appetites leave behind ghosts.

Today her violence has left nicks in the hardwood floor, a bit of sand scattered about and always the sewage smell of the ocean. The nicks and the mess and the odour will go when I go. The ghosts are only for me.

Dad digs out by the leaning fence post in the salt brine air of Largs Bay and hollers at Mum for a beer.

'Mum's sleeping,' I say as I heave my back against the sagging corrugated iron, careful not to put too much snarl in the words. It's a knife-edge mood kind of day for Dad. You need to feel it out, sentence by sentence, until the knife falls definitively one side or the other. 'You know she only just got back from the hospital.'

The iron creaks but doesn't budge.

'Damn fuckin' fence. One day we'll be up the coast there, in Brighton, with them no-seaweed beaches and them rich oceans.'

He says *one day* like he does more with his days while I'm at school and Mum's working than just sit and drink and complain about the government. In the scrub further down the fence line, Sandpiper eyes Dad suspiciously, readying herself to swoop if he steps a boot too close to the nest she's got camouflaged low beneath the sea brush.

'Pretty sure it's all the same ocean, Dad.'

'You smell this shit, then go stick your face in them Brighton waters, come back and tell me it's the same bloody ocean!'

The pickaxe makes a dull thud in the sandy peat as Dad slams it down. Sandpiper bristles and inches closer to her nest. She's been there for weeks now, building and layering her nest, and Dad, for all his birdwatching nonsense, hasn't even realised. I hold on to this little secret I share with the sandpiper, relishing in the deep privacy of it all. I creak against the fence and the wind creaks it back. The smell of sausages cooking on the Weber next door competes with the whiff of seaweed dunes. The pickaxe thuds and then I feel the iron shove at my spine. I stumble forwards. My foot catches in the trench Dad has cleaved and I go down just as the whole corrugated fence panel tips forward in a rending groan, stopping just before it can flatten me. My heartbeat reverberates fast and violent through the earth.

There's a moment of silence and it's that knife-edge choice again. We could either laugh at our luck, or Dad goes to that bitter blight of anger he nurses high in his chest. His laboured breaths come sharp.

My ankle has twisted and I can't pull it out from between the earth and the fence. I'm stuck prone on my stomach on the ground, holding the black, slitted gaze of the sandpiper in the shadows.

'Get up,' Dad says.

'I can't. My ankle's stuck.'

'Get up.'

I wrench my ankle savagely out from under the fence and cast the pain off as something to worry about later. Slowly, Dad hefts the pickaxe. And then he yells and swings it down on the iron fence, the impact resonating through the neighbourhood. He does this over and over. Had I still been on the ground, I might have seen the resolve build in Sandpiper's eyes, or perhaps the instinct-like fear that spurred her into action, or else watched her nod calmly as though she knew it would come to this. I see her explode out from the brush in a flurry of wings and swoop at my father's back, ducking and diving and each time her feet coming a hair's breadth from his skin as he in turn swings the pickaxe down on the fence and yells. I feel the vibrations of the impact through the balls of my bare feet like small earthquakes. Amidst the cacophony, Sandpiper's wings are fast and messy, but silent.

Her little chest makes barely any sound as Dad's axe connects and rends it in two. The axe thuds into the earth, Sandpiper's small body framing it on either side, wings outstretched and bloodied.

Dad sniffs. 'Damn fuckin' bird.'

In my dream, Sandpiper leads me to the door in the floor that lifts open to the Hilliers' wine cellar and piled at the bottom of the stairs are three limp bodies, all with my father's face. They lie ungracefully, limbs askew, eyes replaced by the dark, keen slits of a sandpiper.

'Look. I'm making a hill,' Sandpiper says. 'It'll be a gift for Dad. What do you think?'

I wake up and feel my heartbeat disappear into the memory foam. Outside, Sandpiper hops about by the mandarin tree in the afternoon sun, the light catching the orange-gold feathers in her hair. She gives the ball in her hand, lightly streaked with blood, one last look, before popping it quietly back over the fence.

Moth

Wendy Guest

I might have been better prepared if I hadn't been nauseous from compacting wild grief into grey-suited composure. His widow, Mary, stood at the open door of the chapel, a straight-backed shadow greeting the slow line of departing mourners. There was no other exit. I reached the threshold with its welcome rush of cold air, took a generous lungful and reached for her gloved hand.

She gripped both of her hands into one tight fist at her sternum and leaned in close. 'You're a grub,' she spat it in a whisper from underneath her black cloche.

It wasn't the epithet I'd expected. 'How could you?' would have been right on script. 'Bitch,' entirely appropriate. 'Asshole,' not out of the question. But 'grub' was such an old-fashioned smear, something from my father's generation, back before profanity was quotidian. And that, perhaps, was why it slapped so hard. My father might have called me a grub himself.

I had been keen to mix again with the elite of my discipline at the wake but, knowing she knew, I left at once. I walked away from the stuffy chapel, away from the tedious recitation of his successes and subdued tittering over his good-humoured ways, from the oppressive lilies trumpeting our loss—from the shock of knowing she knew. One or two in the grey-haired clutch of academics under the portico beckoned to me. Friendly faces of former colleagues with appropriately restrained smiles. They were the few people left who understood my decades of devotion to the moth. But I was retired from science. I grabbed my mobile as if it hummed with the most important call in the world and waved them away.

It could have remained our secret, but he had to go and die on me. Well—thank goodness—not *on* me as such ... and yet. I have thought more than once about how I might have held his body and communed with his spirit if I'd been there in the moment he left. He gave me that idea, of course. All the best ones were his. Holding his body as it cooled would have felt more of a slipping away than a slamming shut. But if he'd died at an obvious 'scene of the crime' with me the only living witness, we would have become notorious at the worst time. It was bad enough later, when she exhumed supplementary sympathy from his death by suggesting he'd betrayed her. In the carelessness of a long, tired marriage, he had left behind a trail of breadcrumbs the size of golf balls. Letters. Hotel bills. Professionally he was careful, but personally?

When we first met, I was on the softer path of choosing one of the social ologies: psychology, sociology, even anthropology as I flailed through the early years of university. He lured me into the lab after I turned up to volunteer for something or other. He was the junior professor, me the student. He called me Lolita, which was close enough to Loella. I'd always longed for more basic nomenclature, but my parents were 'creative.' Intellectually, biology hardened me up. Such glorious precision in organic profusion. I found the crisp edges of data-driven results as neat as his bed sheets, meticulous thanks to his army training.

The boundaries of my world became the bush and the lab, his research and his presence. He wanted more. Of course he did. When he left me, I still had the bush and the lab, a stable professional life, and a love life that adhered to the scientific method.

Hypothesis: I'm not much good at it.

Experiment: get married.

Result: divorce.

Replicate.

Discussion: hypothesis confirmed.

Conclusion: I'm not much good at it.

I expected it was my obsession with moths that made me unlovable. At parties, when asked the standard question and I answered lepidopterist, the conversation lasted less than a minute.

'What's that?'

'Study of moths.'

'Interesting. Excuse me, I need another drink.'

Some of those asking knew the word. Those with a literary bent leapt to Nabokov. Those leaning to the aesthetic frothed over their favourite butterfly.

'I study moths.'

'Interesting. Excuse me, I need another drink.'

Moths disappoint people. Chew their clothes, cocoon in their organic almond meal, leave a dusty schmutz when squished and are, mostly, dowdy. Butterflies only disappoint by being too flighty and frivolous for people to get a good look at their gorgeousness. Science itself can be a dry old enterprise to outsiders. And moths? They don't have the glamour of their colourful cousins. No chance of earning the Attenborough-bestowed cache of, say, the charismatic megafauna. And yet I thank the big beasts, and Attenborough of course, for putting extinction on the agenda. Even if no one mourns lost moths.

I will say to my grandchildren, if I live long enough to know them as adults, that they must avoid their first love, no matter what. If they find these pages—if it's you, my dear ones, reading these words— here's grandma's advice: when it comes to your first lover, think of them as an actuary might. They are a pre-existing condition, disqualifying you from any and all reparations. No policy can mitigate the seeping of old wounds from decaying cracks in the heart. There's no insurance against being the worst of fools: an old one. A faded moth to an old flame. A collection of clichés.

Tom called me, after many decades of silence, on the day after my 60th birthday. It's true, as the physicists insist, there are quantum worlds of parallel universes. One plane of existence still held the giddy young woman I had been so long before. She stepped from her alternate dimension into my body in the breath between his 'Hello, Lolita' and my 'Oh.'

He recommended I join a team of retired biologists being recruited to probe the secrets of my beloved scribbly gums. He'd remembered. I was keen to get back into the lab, back to the minuscule magnificence of the images from the scanning electron microscope. There were five of us, early-60s to mid-80s. We discovered more than anyone expected. A clutch of new species, direct DNA links to Gondwana, the unique relationship between moth and tree. I should say it was the chance of deep exploration that motivated me. But I simply wanted to go bush with him again, to see if we could walk as easily, laugh as freely. Did he still pinch the tip of his nose before saying something decidedly unscientific?

Moths can be identified by their genitalia. A scribbly gum moth has all the apparatus for digestion, elimination, and procreation in a body smaller than the length of my little fingernail. The female has ovaries, eggs, a chamber for collecting sperm—all in a space as small as the pin-prick freckles he still had on his shoulders. Their total wingspan is the diameter of a Lifesaver.

Avoid old flames I will say. Childhood wounds scab and teenage traumas scar and our adult bodies grow over the hurts carved beneath ageing skin. Let them sink into the years with grace. Leave them be. Being in love for the first time is the best of drugs. It fixes everything. Each moment together has the depth and height and breadth of all possibilities. Transcendence on two feet. Enjoy it, and let it go. Your first love is a single glass slipper, it sparkles only on the one who fits it to perfection, before they turn you into a toad.

'Mary doesn't want to talk about death at all,' he said once, in a Hilton or Sheraton, the morning sun deepening the ridges and silvering the bristles on his face.

'What if you woke this morning and I was dead?' I asked.

'I'd have to go down for breakfast alone,' he said, stroking his nose.

I pulled the white hairs on his chest.

'I think,' he said, turning serious in a breath, 'I might hold your body for a while, keep it warm and talk to you as you went away.'

'You believe in a soul?'

'If it was good enough for Einstein ...'

'I can't look at a micrograph,' I said, 'at the replication of life in miniature, over and over, without thinking it's all miracles.'

Mary, he said, wouldn't talk about death because she wanted to be 'positive.'

'She says "We're still young at heart!" as if the heart was the only organ of relevance in our mortality.'

He told me he'd had hepatitis, kidney stones, pancreatitis and pleurisy over the years, he knew his organs. Our hearts were a lifetime away from young, but we had shared them when they were. Nostalgia hoodwinked us into believing the creaking, leaking, broken old things they'd become still had some latent vigour.

'Life!' he said, often. 'It's gonna kill me.'

I will also say—if ever I am asked for advice—that a common language of fascination, a shared interest, makes for a strong bond. I could tell him the ovipositor has slender apophyses and membranous ovipositor lobes, closely appressed, and with scattered bristles, rarely sclerotised, spinulose and posteriorly oriented, and he would know I was describing the genitals of the female *Ogmograptis scribula* and not *Ogmograptis racemosa*. A strange substitute for talking dirty perhaps, but there is nothing sexier than being understood.

He wanted a cardboard coffin and no cemetery. He said he wanted to feed the scribbly gums with his own carbon. He turned to me and swept the hair from my face. My head knew he was seeing every sagging wrinkle and the odd stray whisker but my heart, which was the only organ of relevance for *me* just then, felt immortal. He didn't get cardboard. He got the whole glossy, silver-furnished, walnut-polished catastrophe. Burned by non-renewable fossil fuels. I don't want to know what she did with his ashes.

The funeral came back to me today—was it two years ago?—because I saw Mary at the theatre last night. Interval. She was with that old hanger-on Bryan Elton, clasping his arm, something Darwinian in the triumphal thrust of her chin as she stepped in front of him (in her nipped-waist, green linen coat dress) as if protecting him from the predator (in her flat shoes, jersey pants and a sweater.)

'Loella,' she said, not a greeting so much as a warning chipped from ice.

What a species. Way past our reproductive years we continue our mating rituals. I'm getting sloppy. I see I just superimposed competitive human cultural drives onto Darwin's purer theory. But anthropomorphism is, well, human. After a few awkward words, Mary turned and stalked away. Elton followed, glancing over his hunched shoulder like an old dog caught with a scrap of heirloom lace in his mouth.

Walking to the scribbly gums this morning, I had little memory of the second half of the play, only that it was sad. After the funeral, Elton called me once, asking to take me for a drink, or dinner. He had no interest in my counteroffer of a bush walk. He probably thought I was available for sex, given Mary's revelations of my affair with Tom. I expect he didn't remember I'd turned him down 40-odd years before. Just another swing-and-miss for him. It was both pitiable and oddly admirable, his dogged aspiration to push biology passed entropy—propelled by no more than the enduring engine of ego. It's what we've done with the whole planet, after all.

My father spoke to me this morning, while I was tracing the cryptic script of the scribbly's meandering scars. For decades I have tried to read this inscrutable language. It was for the *Eucalyptus haemastoma* that I chose this piece of land. The trees communicate with me through subtle transmissions. Staring at this one, I might feel a vague pressure that turns my body to the left and there, a pop of yellow marks the first wattle blossom. I feel heaviness and lean towards the ground to find a chrysalis. This tree has even helped me find my keys—I asked, waited, went home and there they were. This morning, as my slow forefinger moved over the braille of the calcified ruts, I heard my father's voice as clear as a magpie's warble.

Better to be curious than cute.

He'd said it to me as a kid.

Why? The universal question of childhood.

Because it makes for a more interesting life.

But can't you be both?

Perhaps some people can ...

Better to be curious, he said again this morning. I think he knew Mary's lovely linen coat dress was still hanging in my mind. Elton's ex-wife, Jean, told me—when I called her to giggle over his offer to date me (do we *never* grow out of this stuff?)—that Mary had intimated Tom's heart attack struck during sex. Unlikely, given his testimony of their marriage, but I felt the stab.

I hope you're not curious about what I'm thinking just now, Dad.

I stared at the scribbles. These days I can see a clear image of the first stage larva, a miniature string of translucent pearls, its clueless wanderings making the first, tentative lines as it chomps through cork cambium. A few millimetres of jelly with the jaws and instinctual imperative to mine almost-solid wood. Through subsequent instars, its pattern settles into strong, zigzagged arcs, sweeping downwards. The loop of its turnaround is a tiny noose, condemning it to retrace its track, chewing over old ground. Back and forth it feasts on the bark's callus and its own frass, growing fat, sprouting nascent legs.

Somewhere—I searched but never found it, not even with the best instruments—is the point where the caterpillar turns its nudging head to the horizontal plane and moves towards its destiny. Little in the research suggested what triggers it. Discomfort in its fattening body? The faint warmth of the sun? We found some correlation with low-pressure weather systems, but whatever the signal, the caterpillar suddenly bores through to the outer bark—sun! air! It drops or crawls to the ground to pupate in the duff, resting as the damp gossamer of wing tissue grows along its resting back. I think it's heroic. And that's anthropomorphic. But I'm a sucker for metamorphosis.

My daughter says come back to the city. Come and spend time with the children. The doctors are better in the city, she says. And, of course, she could do with the help. I get pain, but pain doesn't scare me as much as outliving my natural lifespan. Decay deserves respect, not pills and procedures condemning me to too many years of knowing my best work, and best love, are behind me. My cardboard coffin, my cocoon, is up in the garage. Now science is done with me, my fantasies of what's next are unfettered by constraints of intellectual rigour. If there's a judgment, I hope to see the jury benches crowded with all the extinct creatures we culled or commercialised or crowded out. And if I find it's all very biblical up there, but I still manage to squeeze past the gates, I hope the celestial choir will welcome an uncertain alto, with brownish, grey wings that leave a powdery dust as they brush by the eternal harp.

Ewe

Josephine Browne

The farmer says irritably, 'Leave it.'

She looks down the slope of dust, knobbled with tree roots, to the sludge in the creek. The ewe has fallen off the edge of the concrete overpass near the bank, sliding down to the small pools over shiny, sticky clay. The farmer is leading the rest of the mob on. They turn after the bridge, following the creek bank toward the yawning paddock gate.

The legs of the mob are chaos as they jostle to get away from the barking dog in the rear. Scattered among the boulders of grubby ewe fleece, the white lambs dance to keep up, heads squishing between their mothers' flanks and bellies. Cries issue from pink mouths as the lambs dodge in, scurrying, the bright fluff of their fleece covering gangly legs like new stockings.

The farmer has said more than 'Leave it'—that was his parting shot. He is irritated because the ewes have eaten a weed that has blinded them. He expects it will be temporary, but disabled mothers are the last thing he wants—a nuisance of increased work. It's their own damn fault they have to be moved into a smaller paddock, away from the weed, so when his son's girlfriend cries out that one has fallen, it is just another frustration on a bad day. The new girlfriend is the only one in the house who can help with the blind mob because his son, who once fell into this creek himself, is lying in bed, delirious with fever, and his wife is in town.

'But what will happen?' the girlfriend calls, above the barking dog, the bleating sheep, the talkative lambs.

'The mud'll break its legs. I'll shoot it later.'

The dog is cooperating, but the girlfriend has stalled, staring into the creek bed where the sheep lies, her legs flailing as she tries to stand, bleating urgently as the mob moves away.

At the top of the bank, a lamb pauses, her front legs splayed, her chest low to the ground. The girlfriend hears the lamb reply to the agitated calls of the struggling ewe. The lamb knows, somehow, not to venture down the steep slope, toward the mud where her mother is stuck. She bleats, and her mother's head lifts, her ears twitch, and her neck stretches towards her lamb. With an effort, the ewe rolls, her legs pressing down through the sludge, into the clay. The lamb bleats again. The mother's ears shift toward the sound, her feet fumble for a footing, and she answers, turning her blind eyes toward the top of the bank where her lamb is waiting. The ewe strains as she tries to lift a leg, but she stumbles, falls slowly, and the girlfriend waits to hear the cracking of bones, as the farmer has predicted. The bib of the ewe's fleece meets the creamy mud, a darker patch fingering its way upward as the water seeps into her fleece. Like a hand reaching from the mud, determined to drown her.

The girlfriend looks from the ewe to the farmhouse, where her sick boyfriend lies, to the lamb. She thinks of the story she has heard—a toddler, face down in the mud, still—wonders if she is standing where her boyfriend's mother did, twenty years ago, seemingly looking at death in this creek bed.

The ewe's fleece is taking on water. The side where she lay after she slid, her underbelly and the bib of her fleece are soaking up the creamy sludge, which looks so innocent, a relief among the dusty dry gums and the grit that coats teeth and stings eyes with every breeze. The girlfriend watches as shallow puddles, sparking with sun, disappear around the ewe. Unlike the creek water that once entered the toddler's lungs, the ewe cannot spew this danger from her fleece. The girlfriend thinks of the weight of water, in a baby's lungs, on the ewe's fleece. She feels a rising panic: the farmer is right, the ewe will be shot, because he will not tenderly lift her from the creek bed, the way he did with his son, barking orders to his wife over the frenzied dogs, hunching over the floppy body in the back of the car all that long roaring drive to town, breathing, breathing, breathing. The ewe's legs are not long enough to lift her belly clear of the mud; her fleece absorbs the heavy stickiness. She is imperceptibly sinking.

The lamb baas more urgently, turning her head to where the mob, harassed by the barking dog, stumbles its way toward the gate. Her mother comes alive to reply, her body shifts as she responds. Lifting her bib, dripping with mud, her muscles strain as the ewe makes a whole-body effort, raising and shifting her front feet forward with a squelch, sliding into the mud a few centimetres ahead, and dragging her heaving body toward the bank. She is like a caterpillar in motion, her rear legs dragging excruciatingly slowly through the sludge reaching for her fleece. Her head drops; she rests, panting, her chin kissing the mud's surface.

The girlfriend, straining too, has heard no crack of bone.

The lamb stands alert, looking toward the retreating mob and the farmer shouting to the dog, then back to her mother. Her calls to her mother are an alarm—short, sharp, repeated. At the cries, the panting mother's ears twitch, her head rises, and her blind eyes stare directly at her lamb. She bleats, and her nose dissolves into rivulets of wrinkles as she makes another effort to extricate herself. A front foot emerges, coated in a glistening, orange boot, and she lurches forward, toward the rise of the bank, falling again, so that the fleece of her bib and belly spread; her delicately boned face seems to rest on a raft of fleece. The ewe's eyes close and the lamb dances a few steps at the dusty top of the bank. She bleats, subdued, glancing at the mob again. The first of the group is racing into the paddock, past the farmer standing with his hand on the gate post. The dog, silent, eyes trained on his master, waits.

The ewe's eyes open. She lifts her head from the mud, which slides from the long hairs under her chin. She calls, struggling for a footing. The dry bank is a short distance away, but she cannot see. Although she has crossed the creek many times, she has not done so blind, on the edge of the flock. Guided by the confident cries of lambs, most of the sheep funnelled safely across the slab bridge. The concrete is thick, part of the driveway, and necessary because the creek has gouged a small gorge, subject to flooding. The ewe, blind and jostled, the sound of lambs and barking in her ears, misstepped and stumbled, falling near the bank, sliding over roots and rocks to find herself in the spring sludge that is fast drying to summer dust, where the girlfriend imagines lizards and snakes will bake themselves in the heat of the long days ahead.

Over twenty years ago, two dogs barked by this bridge, jumping from bank to bank over the shining sludge, where the toddler's body was face down in one of the spring puddles. From the farmhouse, another mother heard the frantic barking, registered it suddenly, with shock, allowing something in. She had been searching for her son, calling now with an edge to her voice that frightened her. She had just laid the mic for the two-way radio back on top of the fridge. She had told her husband, the farmer, to come, but he was a distance away, in the back paddock. The dogs were not lying under the veranda where they usually rested when they weren't working. The dogs were barking. The creek.

The kitchen flyscreen slammed as she ran around the side of the house. She saw them, flickers of their jumping bodies, beside the bridge. The dogs were frantic, leaping from one side of the bank to the other, yelping. She's a mother; she knows, as if she can already see him. She was swallowing vomit, the thump of her heart in her ears, her feet sliding on the gravel, and still no sign of the ute. Why was he taking so long? How did the day's gentle morning, her son's pudgy fingers squeezing the biscuit dough, turn to this?

The kelpie—pausing—saw the mother running. He bounded toward her, in a frenzy of barking, angrily or urgently, she could not think, but he skidded as they met, and turned, leaping. She saw his yellowed teeth and wet tongue, then he was beside her as they ran. His company sped her last metres to the bridge, where she almost fell, sickened and panting, looking down at the small shape of her son, his red overalls. He was face down in a clay puddle with the edge of his yellow bib poking out from under his baby cheek. The creek's moisture had seeped into his overalls, rimming them a darker red against the sticky clay. His white-blonde hair was clean, immaculate, falling to either side of his head—and it is this she will remember later, driving the ute like a maniac, while the farmer slid on the backseat, breathing into their son's lungs all the way to town; then waiting at the hospital, avoiding each other's eyes—how clean his hair was, how untarnished, the shining hair of a loved baby, a toddler his parents adored with all their hearts, the first-born son destined to inherit the farm.

Now the girlfriend stands in the same place her boyfriend's mother had paused and listened for the ute. The ewe, where the toddler fell; she will be shot. The lamb stands on the bank looking more at the mob entering the paddock than at her silent mother. In the farmhouse lies the feverish son, whose teeth are pitted, you can see it when he smiles at his girlfriend. The farmer has saved his son's life, all those years ago—the doctor said so—and only his teeth show it. Over the months and years that follow, they emerge, battle-scarred, from his gums as his baby teeth fall out.

The lamb bleats one last time, and her mother rouses herself from stillness and silence, calling back, but struggling feebly now against the encroaching weight of fleece, the sucking mud. The other mothers, their answering lambs, have slowed and are milling on the lush grass, finding one another. The lambs seek the comfort of suckling, pressing their heads impatiently into their mothers' warm envelopes of fleece, their long tails dancing with pleasure as the milk is let down. The dog turns his head briefly toward the lamb, and back to the farmer, seeking permission. The glance decides the lamb. She turns and runs, runs while the sound of lambs, companions of diurnal frolicking, is strong and clear—safer than her quiet mother, whose silent face lies in the mud, blind eyes unblinking.

As the lamb runs, the girlfriend breathes, 'No.' She has hardly moved, staring as the stains of water and mud on the ewe's fleece grow, knowing that the farmer expects the ewe's leg bones to snap, once they have embedded themselves in the mud. She has heard the story of the creek, all those years ago, of the small toddler body in the red overalls, and the frenzied dogs that alerted his mother. She has heard about the mother's disbelief when she saw how much creek water the baby vomited, spotted with mosquito larvae. The girlfriend has sat silently in the farmhouse, while her boyfriend's mother described waking to check on her son in his cot that night, finding him gone, following the lamplight, finding the farmer. He was holding his sleeping child, silent tears falling on the baby's blanket. At the creek herself now, the girlfriend has watched the blind ewe's response to her lamb. The farmer's wife has already told her that all lamb and ewe cries are distinctive, so they can find one another no matter how large the mob. The girlfriend can see now, as the baaing and responsive bleats settle among the mob, that the ewe in the creek is inert. Her body has weakened with the weight of water.

The girlfriend moves to where the lamb has been. She crouches, stares at the ewe. She voices a mimic of the lamb's call to her mother. The ewe's ears twitch. The girlfriend baas again. The ewe slowly lifts her muddied head, and when the girlfriend mimics the third time, the ewe, her chin just off the surface of the mud, responds, deep and low.

The girlfriend vocalises more urgently. The ewe's ears shift, her blank eyes reach toward the top of the bank, exactly where her lamb stood, blindly meeting the girlfriend's knees. The girlfriend lowers her head and keeps bleating. Suddenly, the ewe is struggling again, hefting against the solid mass of her fleece with her thin legs.

The girlfriend lowers her head, recalling the height of the lamb's face, as she stood with her front legs splayed, calling to her mother. Like an echo of the lamb, she again calls to the ewe.

The ewe's front legs are back up out of the mud, and she is struggling to move forward. She is less than a foot from the dry edge of the bank, but her way is barred by mud, her chin drips blobs of it, and she has a line of wet clay along her fleece like a satin ribbon wrapped around her. As the girlfriend continues to baa, waiting for the ewe's reply and watching her answering effort, the ewe slips twice, and her feet sink back in under her body. The girlfriend strains to hear bones breaking. But at the third attempt, the ewe succeeds in pushing her front feet forward, in using them to heave her weighted body. Her neck strains toward the sound of the baas at the top of the bank.

The girlfriend pauses, allows her a rest, before renewing her bleating cries. The dog, suddenly, surprises the girlfriend, leaning his weight against her, but the farmer calls him off, walking past and across the bridge, calling over his shoulder, 'Fasten that gate when you leave.'

The girlfriend nods, but her eyes stay on the ewe. The ewe is moving forward again, her feet nearing the dry side of the creek bed. She seems to sense a change underfoot—perhaps she can feel the rise of the bank—because this time she doesn't rest, her head doesn't fall onto the mud, although she is panting hard now against the sodden drag of her fleece.

Buoyed, the girlfriend commences a gentle continuous bleating, urging the ewe on. The ewe responds, her muddy front legs emerging again from the mud, finally finding the dark patch of earth that is already forming a crust, baking in the sunshine. Globs of mud fall from her legs, smearing her fleece, as the ewe heaves forward again. At last the girlfriend can see her back legs emerging, stronger now, because her front legs are on the rocky slope, where gum leaves lie in the dips of evaporated pools, and tree roots and pebbles provide the pathway out.

The ewe struggles forward, and the girlfriend stands slowly, moving toward the paddock gate, a hundred yards along the creek bank. Now she is clear of the clay, the ewe steadily climbs the bank, mud blobs trailing her. She is panting with the effort, the weight, but she comes on, without pause, sure-footed, as though she can see now, continuously calling back to the cry of her lamb, issuing from the girlfriend. The ewe manoeuvres with confident steps the familiar rocks and roots of the creek bed she has known since birth, in its meander through the farm's lower paddocks.

As the ewe reaches the top of the bank, the girlfriend glances back towards the mob, quietly eating or resting now. The ewe trots forward, eagerly calling her lamb. The girlfriend guides her with her voice, away from the dangerous bank, toward the shading trees lining the paddock fence.

Finally, the girlfriend reaches the gate, where she lifts the rusted chain from its metal hook and uses her whole body to push the gate wide, her back against the railings, still calling to the ewe. The ewe bounds forward, still bleating, responsive to her lamb's cry.

Groups of lambs are lying, brighter than ever in their freshness, against the green of the grass. One stands nearby, alert, and the girlfriend, seeing this, stops vocalising as the ewe clears the yawning arc of the gate, slowing uncertainly.

The lamb baas and jolts into a crazed run at her mother. The ewe turns toward the sound, head high. She stumbles in her haste, a muddied mess with edges of the sludge already drying crisp in the sun. The girlfriend watches their blissed collision, before putting her hand to the gate.

The Egg

Gabriella Munoz

Women in my family do not believe in colicky babies. For them, babies who cry are sick—end of discussion. If the GP disagrees and refuses to give them antibiotics to make sure the baby gets well and sleeps all day long, as children under six months of age should, they resort to three remedies that have worked as a treat for several generations of Navarros.

The first remedy is a concoction made with cow's milk and lemon, which aids digestion. The second is fancier and includes brandy. The mother must soak her index finger in the sweet amber liquid and rub it on the baby's gums to help the little one sleep. The third is a *limpia*.

When my sleep-deprived mother went to *abuela* Aurora's house holding a tiny screaming baby wrapped in pink swaddles, *abuela* knew something was wrong. My mum, *al borde de las lágrimas*, pleaded to her *mamá* to please fix the child.

'*Pero voy a necesitar ayuda mija. Y ella, mi hermana.*'

'*Ta bien, ta bien,*' said my *mamá*, trying to forget how much she detested her *tía* who had the *descaro* of wearing white on her wedding day. '*Nada es para siempre. Not even viejos rencores.*'

My mum left when *abuela* Inés arrived surrounded by cigarette smoke and holding sage and her old *lupa*. 'I need to sleep,' I imagine her saying between yawns. 'Whatever it takes, but she needs to stop *mamá. Que deje de berrear.*'

After close examination, the sisters decided it was time to cleanse me. The sexagenarians put me in my pram and took me to the market to buy pink roses, fresh eggs and salt. On the way home, they stopped by the local church to fill a flask with holy water. My crying, the background for these activities, didn't bother them; they were on a mission—to fix me. And they had to be quick.

Once home, the old women proceeded to remove my pink swaddles and fill the kitchen sink with warm water, rose petals and a few drops of holy water. Then they gave me a long bath while humming those tunes whose names I don't know but now also hum to myself and my child. My *abuelas* didn't want to leave my skin squeaky clean but to get rid of *el mal de ojo*, the curse that made me cry all day. When they finished, they laid me on the bed, one woman gently pinning me down, the other using her wrinkled right hand to rub the egg's cool shell against my skin and brown hair for several minutes until it had removed all traces of black magic. Then they dressed me in a white sleepsuit and placed me on my grandma's bed, where I slept, they say, for about three hours. My skin fresh. My body, I imagine, finally relaxed, free from the constraints of the cot, the pram or my *mamá*'s rocking arms.

Years later, the two *abuelas* told me over coffee that they summoned my *mamá* before putting the contaminated egg in a glass of water with salt. It didn't sink, they say, but when they cracked it open, the yolk was black. The evil eye had been successfully removed from my pink, plush body. I've always wondered who placed all those dark energies on me. I was just a baby, *inofensiva*.

My *mamá* says that after the egg *limpia* I started sleeping through the night, and I believe her, but every time my *abuela* Aurora told me this story, she would smile and end up with the same sentence: 'There was nothing wrong with you, *mi amor*, you just needed time with your *abuelas*.'

High-Quality Individuals

Ruth Armstrong

Mum reckoned the guy at our hotel bar looked like a young Tim
Winton. It was one of her more random observations but, to be
fair, she was pretty excited. We all were. We'd finally made it to
Western Australia, a satisfying tick on my list of Australian states
and territories, Dad's chance to live out his manly outback fantasies and Mum's pilgrimage to Winton ground zero. Mum loves
old Tim. Last holidays, when we stayed in a place with no TV, she
decided to entertain us by reading *Island Home* aloud in her slow,
monotonous voice. We fell asleep five nights in a row a few pages
into the first chapter.

   Bar-man Tim Winton was called Mike. He was average height
with a round, tanned face, sad eyes and long, dirty blonde hair pulled
back in a ponytail. He was actually a top bloke. Seemed genuine. He
gave me that knowing look that I get from a lot of dudey guys these
days. The one that says, *Not much longer mate. Pretty soon you'll be
free to work the bar or the coffee machine somewhere cool. Hang in
there, brother. It's gonna be awesome.*

Mike turned out to be the main man at the Coral View Family Hotel. He got us all a drink, took our lunch order and checked us in. He even came out beside the dining deck soon after our burgers arrived and kept us company with his leaf blower.

When we'd finished eating, I decided to go for a bit of a look around, leaving Dad free to drag our bags up the rusty staircase to our room.

'How much are we paying for this place?' I heard him ask Mum as he passed her with the first load. 'Looks like it'll blow into the bay in the next decent cyclone.'

I went into the office to see about the wifi and noticed the big screen in the bar.

'You guys ever put the cricket on?' I asked Mike.

He handed me a little voucher with the wifi password on it. 'If someone asked we would. Like cricket, do ya?'

'Yeah.'

'Play?'

'Not this season ... didn't make the team.'

The crinkles around Mike's eyes got deeper. 'Can't ya play on another team?'

'Yeah, but not with my mates.'

'That's no good.' He seemed decently sympathetic. 'Haven't played much cricket. Looks fun but.'

Unlike Dad, I loved the Coral View on sight—from the deep end of its swimming pool to the tip of its satellite dish. I imagined myself settling in for a lazy week of hotel time punctuated by the odd snorkel in the bay. Unfortunately, my travelling companions had other ideas.

It was still dark the next morning when I woke to the sound of the kitchen tidy bin spinning across the room.

Dad sat on the end of my bunk and rubbed at his big toe. 'Morning, Jack. You're up early. Sunrise beach walk?'

It was hard to stay grumpy as the three of us made our way down the short path to the beach in the pink light. We followed the water line around the bay and saw dozens of stingrays lying in the shallows. At their smallest they were the size of dinner plates, their delicate purplish flaps lifting slightly when the waves disturbed them. The ones that saw us darted away to deeper water, leaving imprints of themselves in the sand.

We picked our way over some rocks and came to a lagoon with a narrow channel at each end. A sign in the sandhills said it was a shark nursery and pretty soon we found a pod of those babies. They were not much more than a metre long, glossy black with silvery dorsal fins. We waded in and watched a group of four or five swimming in a tight circle, then legged it to shore when one broke rank and headed straight for us.

At the end of the bay, we came to a sandy point where a sign in the dunes read *Maud Sanctuary Zone*.

'This is it!' Mum was quivering with excitement as she swiped at her phone to bring up the camera. 'This is the place where developers were about to put a dirty big marina and resort back when you were little, Jack, and Tim Winton stopped it.'

We looked down the long, empty stretch of beach.

'I seem to recall he had help,' said Dad, 'from all round the country.'

'Of course,' said Mum. 'He'd never take sole credit for saving Ningaloo Reef, but if he hadn't been so good at describing the landscape maybe nobody would've cared what happened over here. Sometimes the pen is mightier than the bulldozer, you know.'

Back at the town beach we went for a snorkel. The water was clear and cool, and the sand dropped away quickly to a sub-aquatic world of bombies, shallow caves and crevices. Parrot fish chomped on the blue branch coral, silver-white angel fish zoomed around, powered by barely visible vibrating fins, and mudskippers scooped up and spat out sand. There were cleaner fish, long, slim garfish and sparkling shoals of tiny, colourful fish going about their days. I hovered above them in my slow-breathing, goggle-and-snorkel bubble, feeling like an intergalactic spy.

We were starving when we finally dragged ourselves up the beach. Dad and I went to check on the cricket and Mum volunteered to go to the bakery. She returned looking wildly excited. The baker, who reportedly looked uncannily like a fat Tim Winton, had given her a mud map with directions to a place that he reckoned was the best spot for fish diversity in the entire Ningaloo reef zone. Oyster Bridge, he'd assured her, was just 12 kilometres north of our current location, easily accessible by four-wheel drive. Before I'd swallowed my last mouthful of sandwich, Mum had loaded the snorkelling bag and was standing at the door jangling the car keys.

Normally I would protest at being dragged away from the cricket and out into the heat but, to be honest, the test match was shaping up to be crap. Australia was trouncing the Windies in front of a bored-looking crowd over in Hobart, and they weren't being very good winners. It was capping off a year of sledging and poor sportsmanship from the Aussie team. Their current score on my High-Quality Individual count was a fat zero. Always the optimist though, I wondered if that night's 20-20 match in Sydney might be a bit more inspiring. On the way out of the compound, I got Dad to pull up at the office.

Mike sauntered over from the bar. 'Going out?'

'We're off for a snorkel at some oyster place. Just wondering though, any chance you'd screen the Big Bash tonight?'

'Done,' said Mike. 'See ya later.'

Mum said she felt carsick as soon as we left the tar. She handed the map back for me to navigate, and I realised we were in trouble. There was an easy way to Oyster Bridge—down the signposted track to Maud's Landing, then a leisurely few kilometres' drive along the beach—but the baker had ruled it out due to turtle nesting season. Instead, he'd indicated that we should go most of the way along the single, rutted, inland track, then make a clean left-hand turn through the sand hills to reach the spot. It was nice in theory but, in reality, the area behind the dunes was like one big dirt bike course with a tangle of trails heading in all directions. We followed a few that ended either nowhere or back on the main track, then decided to go straight ahead until a definite turnoff became apparent.

It was frustrating but not unusual for the three of us to be bumping along aimlessly and we resorted to form. Mum suffered her carsickness in silence, apart from the odd gasp when the car lurched, and Dad and I talked cricket. We cycled through stats and teams and captaincies and coaches, everything except the elephant in the room—my own epic failure to make the Inner West Under 15As. Not much to discuss, I guess, after my performance in last year's final, but part of me wanted to hear him say it was stupid and unfair that they'd dumped me. The coach reckoned it wasn't my prerogative to walk when I was the team's last hope, but I knew I'd nicked that ball. It was a no-win situation.

After what seemed like miles, the track petered off into a deserted campsite on a shallow weedy bay. We stopped the car and wound down our windows, got a salty whiff of the 42-degree air, then wound them up again. I was ready to give up, but they wouldn't have it. Apart from anything else, Dad was enjoying the off-road driving a little too much, given his skill level. He did a neat doughnut, pointing us back the way we'd come, and we resumed our quest.

We left the main track and floundered around in the maze of trails through the dunes, wheels spinning and chassis veering until the inevitable happened. We rounded a corner, hit soft sand, lunged to the left and ended up stranded on two wheels. We clambered out and stood together, staring at the axle with the smell of the gearbox burning in our throats. Dad spoke first.

'We'll dig her out.'

So we dug, Dad and I, using our upper bodies to rake sand from under the car. We dug until the sand was in all our clothes—clinging to our hair and up our noses—then stopped and rocked the car. When the wheels seemed almost on the sand, we put strips of shrubbery under them and tried to drive out of it but, whatever we did, the vehicle didn't move.

We gave up. Dad stood in his soaked T-shirt with his hands on his hips, staring the car down like it was a baddie in an old Western movie. He turned to Mum. 'Never trust a fat baker.'

That sent them both off—Dad laughing at his own joke and Mum almost snorting the last of our mineral water out through her nose—but I was done. My head ached from the heat and glare. While I was digging, I'd had visions of my friends—the ones who'd stayed home after school broke up to do piano exams, go to sports clinics or have braces fitted—just going about their mundane days in rainy Sydney. Lucky bastards.

'Did either of you bring a phone?' I asked coldly. Mine had been out of service since we'd left the main road.

Dad stood with his hands in his empty pockets, looking guilty, while Mum found hers. It was almost out of charge and showing SOS, but at least she'd saved the number of the Coral View.

We struggled to the top of the highest dune and, standing on tippy-toe with the phone angled just so, I got a bar of service. After a few rings, I heard Mike's voice on the other end—only problem was he couldn't hear me. I hung up and called back twice with the same result before the screen spiralled to black.

We flopped down on the sand. The sun was level with our faces now and I tried not to think about how dry my mouth felt. Out in the bay, the water was at least four different shades of blue against the palest of skies. On a distant sandbar, a flock of seagulls rose together in a white cloud.

'This place is amazing,' said Mum. 'Just like the cover of Tim Winton's *Island Home*. Y'know he saved Ningaloo from the developers a few years ago. Led a big citizen's movement that went global.'

Dad and I glanced at each other.

'Might as well stay here till it cools off,' Dad said. 'Tide's going out. If I can get down the bottom, I can walk around the beach into town.'

We sat in silence as the landscape was transformed by orange-gold light. I began to shiver. Sunburn can do that to you as it gets dark, but I was also scared. Stories of families lost in isolated places circled ominously in my mind. I guessed we could all make it back to town on foot if we had to, but we had an ordeal in front of us and plenty of opportunity for something else to go wrong.

In the moments before the sun deserted us, the broadest dune, off to our left, fired up like a spot-lit stage and onto that stage drove an old white ute. A guy got out and waved and we jumped up and gesticulated back frantically. Mum even managed a scratchy *coooo-eeee*. He hopped back in and drove out of sight, then popped out again on the main track and made his way up to our stranded car. Our rescuer introduced himself as Smiley, and when his companion shuffled over to the driver's side of the ute and gave me a wave, I saw it was Mike.

Smiley worked fast, tying a snap-strap to the front of our car before Dad had even finished telling him the sad story of our afternoon. He signalled to Mike and the ute surged forward, lifting the car effortlessly out of its premature grave. Mum cheered.

'How much?' said Dad.

Smiley lived up to his name, revealing surprisingly white teeth.

'Two hundred and a slab'll do it ... back at the hotel. There's an ATM in the bar.'

I accepted Smiley and Mike's offer of a lift back to town. We drove in companionable silence, watching for kangaroos in the dusk, until we came to the familiar turnoff to Maud's Landing.

'Down there,' said Mike, 'is where they were going to build a big resort. It would've been shit but it didn't happen.'

I waited for him to mention Tim Winton, but he just sniffed and ran his hand through his fringe, keeping his eyes on the road.

'Nobody here wanted it,' said Smiley. 'We made that pretty clear.'

The inside of the ute smelled like my Uncle Jim's office—boozy and sweaty with a touch of unemptied bins—and I had one of those rare moments of feeling totally happy and in place. I couldn't imagine either of these guys in cricket whites, but I knew I was in the presence of high-quality individuals.

Smiley dropped us off in the hotel carpark.

'Thanks for the rescue,' I said to Mike as he slid the office door open.

He shrugged. 'Thanks for the hang-up calls. Took me a while but I figured it had to be you lot.'

He went to go inside, then turned back.

'You bring your cricket gear on this holiday?

'Just a beach set.'

'How about a hit tomorrow arvo? Show me a shot or two?'

Back upstairs I saw that Mum had a copy of *Island Home* by her bed. The cover really did look like the view we'd seen from the top of the dunes. I turned on the TV. The Australian team was celebrating yet another day of crushing the Windies. The test was as good as over.

That night in the bar, Mum reckoned we were served by three Tim Wintons, which was pretty imaginative seeing one of them was an Italian backpacker. Smiley was partway through a beer when we got there. He gave Mum and me a quick salute from the other side of the room as Dad handed him the cash. The Big Bash match was playing on the screen in the bar as promised, but we went to bed early, tired and a little woozy from the afternoon's exploits. I closed my eyes and the scenes played out: the soft, white sand hills rolling back from the shore, the parallel fish universe in the bay, pods of baby reef sharks swimming in the shallows, the smudging of blues where the sea met the sky.

I thought about old Tim. No wonder he stuck up for Ningaloo when people wanted to trash it. All those years, writing all those words that influence how the rest of us feel about wild and natural places made him the perfect man for the job. And Smiley and Mike, knowing every inch of this place, ready to lend a hand and to quietly take the piss, happy in their own leathery skins. It came to me that the lucky people are the ones who get to make their mark in the world just by doing what they love. And I thought about cricket. Don't get me wrong, there was no way I was giving up my dream of making it onto my own high-quality individual list, but I decided that, if the A's didn't need me, I'd find a slot in a team that did.

I was jolted out of my thoughts by the sound of Mum's book dropping on the floor in the next room. The crack of light disappeared from under their door and I lay still, soaking up those first moments of darkness before your eyes adjust and the shadows appear.

Mum wasn't quite done for the night though.

'G'night, Jack,' she called out. 'That Smiley bloke turned up at the right time. Quite a character, don't you think? Looked a bit like a drunk Tim Winton.'

Settling

Andrew Drummond

Despite all the trouble and delays—as if the world's conspiring against him again—Tate makes it with some time to spare. He turns the stereo off but keeps the engine running, takes a moment to gather himself. Long, steady breaths.

He's parked close enough to see his girls coming, but not so close that all the mums on the school run will notice him. A bloke at the end of the school day is an unusual thing. No judgement in that, just stating a fact.

Between the peeling trunks of a row of paperbarks, Tate watches the crossing guard. She's putting her banners out, guiding them through slots in the wooden posts that mark the crossing. With their red and white stripes, the posts remind Tate of boiled lollies.

The crossing guard wears a long jacket—hi-vis, fluorescent yellow, bright orange sash—and a matching hat. Sunlight catches the polished edge of the warning whistle she's hung around her neck.

When the sisters come, Cassidy is striding ahead of Olivia. Always leading, bossy and proud and protective.

It's a farmhouse outside Bendigo. A friend lent it to Tate. 'For as long as you need.'

The property is large and sounds nice. Open space, grasslands, a couple of dams. The perfect place to get away from it all.

Tate hasn't seen it yet. The first time will be with his girls.

It feels like they've grown. Maybe it's the uniforms. He's still not used to seeing Ollie that way. *A second ago*, Tate thinks, *I was holding a baby wrapped in a blanket. Now it's a school dress.*

That's what it's like when you work blocks and miss most of your access visits.

Tate remembers his mate, Coona Pete, born February of a leap year. The 29th. He'd joked about it in the speech he gave at Pete's fortieth. Had said, 'I may be pissed, but by my reckoning, tonight's party is for a ten-year-old. Only slightly more mature, old mate.' Most of the guests had laughed and charged their tinnies. Laughed again as he spotted Pete's wife and said, 'I don't see you arguing, Sue.'

It's like that, Tate thinks. *Or dog years.*

The girls are close. Tate starts winding down his window. He's planned another speech, rehearsed it on the way over. But now the girls are in front of him and he can feel a heaviness on his tongue, the weight of all he wants to say.

Cassidy looks up first and recognises the car. She jumps straight in. Ollie follows like a puppy, flopping onto the back seat, giggling. Tate watches her in the mirror. Tiny, pink fingers buckling her seatbelt. Then he takes off.

Thinking about dams and grasslands and acres of open space reminds Tate of his cousin's farm. It had a dam as well. As kids, he remembers his cousin yelling, 'Dad's filled it with yabbies. We can go yabbying.'

Tate was scared of swimming in it after that, imagining all those yabbies lurking in the murky water, waiting to pinch him.

But not the other kids. They dove right in, splashing around and swimming to a mound of grassy earth in the middle of the dam, climbing onto it with arms raised like kings. Tate had watched them from the muddy bank.

'Come on, Tate,' the others called.

'I'm all right.'

After they went back to their game, he finally took a step, his foot instantly sinking into mud. He'd taken a couple more steps when he felt the pinch—quick and sharp. He lifted his leg. There was a nick in the thin cord of flesh above his heel. A line of watery blood leaked out and he watched it run over his skin. The red drip of it into the dam.

He had pushed off the bank at the sight of it, heart racing, and collapsed into the water.

When the others got out, he kept swimming. 'You wouldn't go in,' someone said, 'and now you won't get out.' Tate didn't respond. What could he say? That he was scared of the bank, scared of getting pinched again.

Sitting here with his girls, years later, he thinks of his scar. A smooth white ripple on the surface of his skin. That pinch had seemed like nothing at the time, a bit of blood, but it has marked him.

Eyes still on the mirror, gaze steady, he watches the last straggle of kids as they walk out the school gates, then he focuses on the road ahead.

The jeans sit in a clump on the passenger seat, T-shirts lying on top of them, shoes and socks on the floor mat. Tate reaches over and grabs the lot, handing it back between the seats. 'Put these on,' he says.

Cassidy says, 'Where?'

Tate realises he hadn't thought of that. The public toilets at the Reserve come to mind, or maybe the footy club. 'On your body,' he says.

Cassidy rolls her eyes and says, '*Da-ad*.'

'Jump in the back-back,' Tate says, 'but not yet. I've got something for you first. A present.'

'A present?' the girls say in unison.

Cassidy leans forward and pokes her head through the seat gap. Tate can sense her eyes on him. 'What is it?'

'That's for me to know and you to find out.'

'*Da-ad!*'

'All right, all right. It's in the back-back. The Kmart bag.'

Cassidy slings back and bounces against her seat, hooks her hand over and loops the bag into the space between her and Ollie. She opens it and takes the hoodies out and checks their sizes, handing the smaller one to Ollie. Both are black. Ollie's has a transfer of a monster truck on it, mostly green, flames bursting from its exhaust. Cassidy's is plain black but with camo sleeves.

'Thanks, Dad,' Cassidy says, ripping at the tag with her teeth.

'Jump in the back-back,' Tate says. 'Get changed.'

The girls take turns. For once, Tate is thankful for his beaten-up station wagon—the one thing he got out of the break. It's saved them from the public toilets.

While the girls change, Tate drives straight to the hairdressers. He parks out the front.

Cassidy says, 'What are we doing here?'

'What do you think?' Tate says. 'Getting haircuts.'

He looks at his girls' doubtful faces in the rear-view mirror.

'Boy cuts, like Katy. We need to look nice for our special weekend. Even I'm getting a haircut.'

The girls seem unconvinced. Eventually, Cassidy says, 'All right, Dad.'

Inside the salon, a teenage girl is sweeping curls of hair off the floor. The other hairdressers are having a conversation. They stop talking when the bell above the door tinkles.

'Come in, come in,' one of them says. 'Do you have an appointment?'

'My girls here,' Tate says, directing Cassidy and Ollie to a couple of chairs at the back of the salon. 'Four o'clock. We're a bit early. I hope that's okay?'

'It's fine. How would they like it?'

'Boy cuts,' Tate says again. 'Like Katy.'

The girls don't say anything. Cassidy has a look on her face. She's watching him in the salon mirrors.

Tate says, 'I'll have a cut, too.'

'We don't do men.'

'Just a buzz cut,' Tate counters, nodding to the girl with the broom. 'She can do it.'

'She's only an apprentice.'

Tate tries to seem cheerful and light. 'It's all practice,' he says. 'As long as you've got clippers, I'm sure she'll be fine.'

The hairdresser shrugs and looks over at the teenage girl, who is panning the last curls off the floor. The girl empties them into a bin, then walks over to the steriliser. A set of clippers sit on its aluminium rack, gleaming blue in the UV light.

At dusk one evening, they'd gone catting. Tate's cousin had held the rifle relaxed against his side, straight up and down, like a professional soldier. Ahead of them, the sky was pink and grey above the horizon, streaky gold in the places it met land.

Tate's uncle was spotting. 'It's not like rabbits,' he'd told Tate before they left. 'You have to hit the spot at the last possible moment. And light up his eyes. A feral outside the spot doesn't exist. If you give him the chance to see it, he's gone.'

Tate remembers the cat looking at them from the distance, struck motionless by the glare. A blast of light encircling its head and shoulders, its eyes glinting yellow-green. The way it had seemed so alone, so singled out.

Moments later, the explosion of the rifle. Still ringing in Tate's ears, it seems, because it's one of the things that's stuck with him.

The girls have started complaining.

'I need a drink, Dad,' Cassidy says. 'I'm hungry.'

In the rear-view mirror, Tate sees her rubbing the back of her neck, still fascinated by the bare skin. 'Don't you have anything in your bags?'

'We ate it all at school.'

Tate pulls into the next rest area. The SES are serving tea and coffee from a van. There's a doughnut truck parked beside them.

Tate buys his girls a bucket of hot chips to share. They start wolfing them down while Tate waits for his coffee. A woman stands next to the girls. Tate watches steam rising from her cup, the way she clasps her hands around it for warmth and blows cooling air over its rim, how the string and tag of her teabag flutter in the breeze. Then he looks at his girls with their hoods pulled up and tomato sauce all over their faces.

The woman says, 'You can take a breath if you want, kids.'

Cassidy and Ollie look up at her blankly.

'You must be hungry,' the woman says, glancing at Tate. 'You're eating so fast.'

'We haven't had anything since school,' Cassidy says, a mouthful of mashy-white potato making her difficult to understand. 'Our Dad picked us up straight after. He's got us for the weekend.'

The woman smiles thinly and says nothing. After a second, she blows more cool air over her tea and takes a slow sip.

Cassidy looks around and lets it all sink in. She says, 'It's like a hideout.'

Tate opens the kitchen cupboards and finds them fully stocked. Good old Davo. 'What do you want?' he says to his girls. 'You can have anything.'

'Anything?' Ollie says.

'Yep,' Tate says. 'Anything.'

Cassidy checks out the cupboards, filled to the brim with tin cans and cartons and brightly coloured boxes covered with images of toucans and monkeys. 'Mum doesn't let us eat this stuff,' she says.

Tate looks at both his girls. 'Well Mum isn't here, is she?' he says.

By the time the girls have finished their cereal, everyone is laughing and cracking jokes. They stack their dishes, then go outside to start exploring. The paddocks out the back are dry and dotted with mounds of earth. Tate walks his girls from burrow to burrow, pointing out the holes where the rabbits enter and exit. Later, they all get into their bathers and go swimming in one of the dams. Tate carries Ollie on his back as if he's a big hippo and she's an elegant bird. Not once does he consider the possibility of yabbies.

After they've all showered, the girls sit on the couch and watch a Disney movie. Tate puts a roll of garlic bread in the oven to heat up while he cooks a big pot of Spaghetti Bolognese. Cassidy calls out when it's almost done. She says, 'That smells so good.'

Tate watches his girls eat. It makes him happy, taking care of them. If only their Mum and the others could see him now. Then they'd know.

As soon as it's dark outside, Cassidy and Ollie start to get tired. Tate goes into the bedroom and pulls down the blankets while the girls brush their teeth. They come in and collapse onto the beds, their eyes heavy, bellies full. Tate tucks them in tight. He stays until they fall asleep, then he slips out of the room and heads to the lounge, flopping onto one of the couches. He lies there a long time, thinking about his girls' breath—the way their bodies rise and fall with it, tucked warm beneath their blankets.

That's when he notices the sound of gravel crunching under tyres and sees the slow flash of headlights across the dining room wall. He gets up heavily and moves to the window, easing the curtains open an inch or two.

White car, blue uniforms.

It's funny how people always think of sirens and flashing lights. More often than not, it's just a gentle roll up a driveway in the dark.

'Dad?'

Cassidy and Ollie are standing on the other side of the lounge, sleepy-eyed. Their short hair is mussed and kinked, sticking out in spikes because the peroxide is still fresh.

'Get dressed, girls,' Tate says. 'It's time to go.'

Inheritance

Atul Joshi

The woman stumbled along the embankment. She hummed a song, moving her head to an invisible beat. On each side, she saw the mirrored surface of the water reflect the massed monsoon clouds in the sky. Angry, rain-sodden, grey pilgrims, on their way from sea to mountain. Their presence turned day into dusk. With each step her breath became more laboured, each gulp of air brought more of the brackish smell, adding to her thirst.

She stopped to drink from her bottle and surveyed the vast delta as it stretched out in every direction. The strip of land she stood on was an in-between space, claimed from the sea in a losing battle with its inexorable rising. When she'd been a girl, this place had been green. Paddies everywhere. Now their land was flooded with saltwater—turning it from rice to shrimp bowl.

A white rag doll in a widow's saree, she carried a chair on her back, tied around her waist with the shawl that would keep her warm in the days ahead. Knotted above the fabric, a strip of blue plastic to keep her dry. In one hand, a tiffin, stuffed with rotis, in the other the water bottle she drank from—easy to refill once the rain starts.

Thirst slaked, she resumed her unsteady walk until she neared the end of the ridge, on the edge of which she saw a solitary boy seated on the muddy ground.

Spooked by the feeling of being watched, he turned and spotted the scarecrow. 'End of the road Auntie.' He thought it strange that she was out alone. 'Nothing more out here.'

She eyed the banks on either side and reknotted her shawl to tighten the chair, before disappearing down the levee.

'Wait ... ' the boy cried out, annoyed at having his fishing interrupted.

She reached the water, half-stumbling, half-sliding down the slope. As she stood ankle-deep in sludge, her saree and shawl now splattered with mud, she realised she'd lost the chain around her neck with its silver pendant.

The boy hurried to where she'd stood. By the time he got there, she'd struck out across the sunken field, no longer alone. As the first rain began to fall, a grey dorsal fin curved out from the water alongside. Dropping his rod, the boy ran home to tell them about the crazy auntie walking on water.

Coming to the end of St Vincent Street, they emerge into George Square. Suddenly, Rahul finds himself surrounded by its self-assured Victorian architecture, monuments to science and culture, tribute to Empire and industry's reach and magnificence. Before Evelyn can lecture him from her guidebook, the crowd pushes them towards the stage.

They'd set out from Kelvingrove Park in what should have been a thirty-minute march. An hour later, the sheer number of people means there's still a throng entering the square. People dressed as dinosaurs and other extinct species, families with dogs, prams, babes in arms, children with painted faces. The colours of their bright ponchos and tartans struggle against the gloomy autumn sky. Almost all are holding white banners on poles, stencilled black letters over which are spray painted sunbursts of highlighter colours, like the one Evelyn's carrying—'Demand Action'.

It'd been a once-in-a-lifetime opportunity. The first in his family to attend college, Rahul wanted to be a poet. One of those revolutionary writers like Roy, Dawesh, or Chourey, part of a lineage back to Tagore.

'Make me the gardener of your garden,' his mother quoted when he showed her his first poems, in the days before her mind began to wander. That started after his father went missing during the first struggle for their land. Left in a state of perpetual bereavement, she turned to her ancestral gods.

'Better to be the gardener,' she later said in a hollow voice, after aquaculture had taken over, 'than the flower that blooms and dies.'

Thrust into the role of carer, he studied food security instead. Their safety was all that mattered. He transformed his poetic fervour into dizzying vertical gardens of green, rebuilding damage into new potential. Accreditation to attend the United Nations Conference of the Parties in Glasgow as a youth delegate followed.

'You've been chosen, *beta*,' his mother said, 'to give Padma her freshwater back.'

The days that followed his arrival in Scotland were a quick slide into disillusionment. He shared a crowded home above a pub next to a petrol station—one of nine squeezed into a four-bedroom rental, an hour's drive from the city. Over take-away, they shared knowledge and ideals, while eating to the beat of bands below. He befriended Evelyn, the geothermal expert from the Pacific, over Pad See Ew.

'I was born in the Ring of Fire,' she said, slurping a noodle. 'The Kermadec Arc. My ancestors have lived with that energy for millennia. Using that heat is my birthright.'

No one at the conference was interested in their science though. Being experts in their fields didn't count for much. Instead of keynotes, they were scheduled to perform songs in national costume.

'What are you going to sing about?' he asked.

'Volcanoes!' she said. 'I'm descended from them and the song is part of my inheritance. How about you?'

'Water,' he said. 'About our great river the Padma.'

'Fire and water,' she laughed. 'The real challenges.'

They waited backstage on their allotted day, while the President of Evelyn's island home relayed a speech knee-deep in water on a beach—beside him, a tube marked out in metre increments the expected sea level rise. As he spoke, water filled it and soon passed his height. Delegates clapped and cheered. Someone who'd been tipped off about the stunt launched a giant beachball. Soon it became a game as the ball was punched around the room. Evelyn's face reflected fury at the disrespect to her elder.

They were finally led on stage after the ball was cleared, order restored. She stepped forward to begin her ancestral song but was cut short when the moderator realised it had ticked past their allotted time. Before anyone in the audience could register their presence, they were ushered off by apologetic faces.

He felt the heat radiating off Evelyn's body into the floor and up his legs.

'It's okay,' he said. 'I'm sure they'll reschedule it.'

'It's too late,' she replied.

Two days later, the frustration of a week of inaction is now reaching its peak in George Square.

'Failure,' he hears the girl say on stage. Her face fills the giant screens either side of her. 'A festival of greenwashing ...'

The rest of her words are lost as the crowd cheers. Phones are held aloft recording this moment, catching every word, image, sound.

Evelyn elbows him and points.

On a mobile screen nearby he sees a news bulletin that stops his breath.

'Three months' worth of rain in twenty-four hours. Thousands missing.'

Footage of flooding, mudslides and submerged towns, villages washed away. He knows those places; he can almost smell the brackish aroma. The bulletin cuts to a reporter. He's standing under an umbrella beside a tarp that's covering something.

The owner of the phone shows it to a neighbour. Soon, people all around are switching to the news broadcast. The girl disappears from the massive screens and the footage everyone is looking at pixelates in panoramic view.

Briefly, something emerges from the water beside the reporter—a reptilian head that just as quickly submerges. It's followed by a flick of a double-finned tail. There's a collective gasp in the crowd.

He grabs Evelyn's arms and drags her away.

'Oh, to what foreign land do you sail?' his mother sang the old Tagore song the night before his departure.

'Come to the bank a moment,' he responded, 'moor your boat for a while.'

'Good *beta*,' she said, smudging a red tika dot on his forehead. 'You've learnt it well. They will listen when you sing!'

He brought his hands together in prayer, bowed his head and bent to touch her feet. As he did so, she slid a chain over his neck. Rising, he felt the pendant hanging from it—an animal with the head of a crocodile and tail of a dolphin.

'It's just like yours,' he said.

'Padma Devi's *makara* will protect you,' she said. 'It will help you conquer fear when you sing the song, when the melody brings the freshwater back.'

'Thank you for teaching it to me,' he said.

'It's your song now too,' she added, stroking his cheek.

It was the pendant he used to talk with her each night. In those moments between wakefulness and sleep, he'd hold it between his lips, and they'd meet in the shade of the mango tree he'd known since childhood, where she sat in her white saree, shelling peas.

'Mummy, there are so many people here!' he said the first night. 'We had a welcome ceremony. I saw all the presidents of the world!'

'*Arre waah*!' she exclaimed, collecting peas that had popped away from the bowl before the chickens got to them.

'They took us on a city tour,' he continued, 'so we missed the first plenaries. So many old buildings and statues.'

'Just rubbish ceremonies, don't mind that!'

'We had our first session,' he reported the next night. 'But no one came.'

'*Buddhuus*,' she said, knocking the bowl of peas over. 'Idiots.'

'Mummy, they are not listening to us,' he said by the third night.

'I will pray to Padma. She will be with you tomorrow, they will listen then. They must listen.'

She did not tell Rahul that, as the boy grew and the water filled with salt, she hadn't found Padma in her prayers for years. And with her, the dolphins that played in these waters disappeared.

'They cancelled the songs,' he finally said.

'You must sing,' she said.

'What? No one's going to listen. No one will do anything.'

'The song will be sung,' she said. 'I will make them listen.'

'What's your name?' the reporter asks her, raising the tarp. Seated, the water's already at her knees.

'Pad ... Pad,' she stutters. 'Padma.'

'Why are you here?'

'To sing our song.'

The reporter's laughter is lost in the sound of falling rain. 'You will drown,' he says. 'It's already risen two inches while I've been standing here.'

'It's clean, fresh water,' she says. 'She's coming to wash the salt away.'

The reporter sways from side to side as the current tugs at his legs. He turns to the camera operator and motions the cutting motion across his neck. '*Vah paagal he*,' he mutters and leaves. 'She's mad!'

Soon after, she sees the whirring of drones above her. She knows her son is watching, but, with her pendant gone, their link is broken.

The flood is now at her chest. The pull of it is so strong that she clamps her hands over the seat's edges. Her weight—what there is of it—wedges the chair's legs in the mud, but it won't hold much longer.

She looks up at the drones.

'Floodwaters twisting and swirling everywhere,' she mouths, slowly tilting her head to the beat. 'On this side a paddy, no one but me ...'

The water covers her mouth. It's flooding her lungs.

She feels a smooth body nudge her. Recognising its touch, she strokes it, hand gliding over slick skin, following the curve of the dorsal fin. She lets go of the chair.

Back in their room, Evelyn boots up her laptop.

They see the waters rise and the reporter leaves. Then the overhead shots, the woman looking at the camera, mouthing words.

'Who is she, Rahul?' Evelyn asks.

'My mother,' he says.

'What's she saying?'

'It's my song, we used to sing it together.'

He barely contains the sobs welling in his throat as he watches the waters rise and cover her.

'She's given you a gift,' Evelyn says. 'She wants you to use it.'

'I can't,' he says.

'A gift like that can't be returned, an inheritance can't be refused.'

'Inheritances are tragedies,' Rahul says. 'They are gifts from the dead or dying. It's not the kind of gift I want.'

She watches him pack his bag in silence.

Evelyn washes her diesel and paint-stained hands, then slides on the flax-weave top. She steps into the beaded skirt and ties it around her waist. Over this, she draws a black, animal-skin cloak. She applies ochre and oils to her hair before inserting the decorative combs made of bone. Instead of the feather headdress she wore at the conference, she places a wreath of greenery on her head.

Downstairs, the pub's packed with locals. She pushes through the beer-drunk crowd to the makeshift stage where tonight's band has set up. Taking the mike, she speaks.

'My people come from volcanoes,' she says.

No one listens.

She tries again, raising her voice. 'This song was gifted to my ancestors in a time of great need.'

Some turn to look at her and laugh, others continue talking.

She intones a sound to get their attention. It's a deep, tectonic note that pours from the subwoofers and flows across the floor like lava. It vulcanises the feet inside their shoes, rises up their legs and into their chests, silences their throats. Later, in the Burns Unit of Glasgow Royal Infirmary, people will recall they wanted to scream but suddenly couldn't.

'It's a song of the asthenosphere,' she continues, 'a ballad of ash and fire.'

Silence falls around the pub.

'If our embers are forgotten and unheeded,' she chants, 'they tend to start fires.'

By the time Evelyn finishes, Rahul's already at Buchanan Bus Station. As he changes platforms, he hears sirens. He looks up, amazed to see the sky has cleared to reveal the colours of sunrise. He checks his watch and knows this is an illusion. It's a false dawn—the flashing lights of fire engines bouncing off the clouds massing in the sky, the glow of a distant conflagration.

He boards the Airport Express. Sitting on the coach while waiting to depart, he watches the TV streaming the national news relay service. As the bus reverses to exit the bay, he sees the firefighters on screen battling flames. Water streams down the brick walls and over the spray-painted graffiti outside the pub, streaking its highlighter colours: 'We are watching you.' Ambulances ferry people away. He rushes up to the driver and makes him stop. Dragging his luggage behind him, he steps off.

The news on screen cuts to the floods. The blue tarp's bobbing in the muddy waters before a drainage sluice sucks it out of frame. The camera pans and focuses on the woman. She's riding a dolphin as it leaps and swims towards the mountains. She's singing.

'Floodwaters twisting and swirling everywhere. I sit on the riverbank, sad and alone.'

Rapunzel, Let Your Hair Down

Mary Winning

In my dreams, the planets collide. The universe implodes, and the sky crashes at my feet. I sweep away the broken pieces and replace the sky with a blue spare, kept behind a photo of my late husband. I like him better dead. Sometimes, when his memory lodges into mine, I visit his grave at the base of the big red hill. Lifting my skirts, I relieve myself near his headstone, which reads: '*Here rests a man who could take the piss*'. Laughing in a wild howling wind, I let my hair down and dance on the earth covering his brittle bones.

It's a large splatter—not neat. The raindrop, heavy, hits the window and spreads across the glass. One of only a few that will fall. The dirt-covered pane obscures the sky. The dry summer wind brings dust and grit to the sill where it stockpiles until the winter rains. The veranda commands the best view for a summer storm. You can feel nature's strength and inhale her scent. An explosion shakes my tower, and the air is sharp with electricity. Tomorrow will be unbearably hot.

The morning births a screeching blue sky. A radiating sun bakes the ground, cracking the ochre dirt into deep crevices, a peril for small insects. Yesterday's storm failed to quench a parched valley, and the sigh of thirst speaks deep in this open auditorium.

White corellas flock to the surrounding ghost gums, screeching warnings of his coming. The black cockatoos gliding above the hills lament his arrival. In brilliant sunlight, he walks out of a red dust cloud spinning across my isolated driveway. He is looking for work.

I tell him: 'You can start tomorrow.'

It is only the vineyard and me. The cry of harvest can be heard in the chorus of fruit-thieving birds and the low resonating hum of the cicadas. Marcu leaves to return the next day at dawn.

Despite the promise of shade, the vineyard offers no respite protecting only an underbelly laden with clumps of swollen purple jewels. Marcu's experienced hands strip the vines of their treasures with ease. Occasionally he stands looking towards the veranda and wipes sweat from his brow. He is a jewel himself: rare, exotic. A foreign prince from another land come to save me. His gentle smile weakens my armour protecting a petrified heart beating under fragile ribs.

My mother abandoned me in this remote, arid land as punishment for letting my hair down, for bearing children with a man who saw me as property and forced me into marriage. My husband is no more. Cursed by blindness, his bones snapped and his teeth rattled as he tumbled down the slope of the big red hill to stop broken at its base. The ground opened, swallowing his body as it did with my daughters. The hill fed on his flesh and, once quenched on his warm sweet blood, the hill trembled and the soil became vibrant.

One cycle of the moon passes. The harvest has ended. An invisible fire radiates over the land, releasing resin from leaves. Hypnotic scents of eucalyptus permeate the air. I sit on the veranda overlooking hills that rise and plummet. Narrow tracks made by grazing animals zigzag across dusty slopes. Marcu leans against a veranda post, his gaze on a distant uninterrupted horizon. My eyes linger on his body, following lines that blend into sensual muscular curves. Sweat beads on hot skin, causing material to stick and cling. A primal stirring awakens within me.

'The land is in heat. One spark of passion will cause an inferno,' I tell him.

A smile twitches on his lips. 'Where is your husband?'

'He is here, buried deep in the earth, under sky and stars.'

A fly tracks a path on my arm. With a quick hand, I end life, watching it spasm in my palm. We stay on the veranda, feeling summer's acerbic burn. Dry wooden posts split in dull bursts; animals remain silent, seeking refuge under shade. A hot wind sears small birds, and they fall to the ground to be feasted upon by snakes, the only things to survive in this furnace with comfort and purpose.

'Tonight, the moon will be full. Sometimes I walk in the silence. Will you come with me, Marcu?'

He nods.

We journey, pausing on the spine of the big red hill taking in an ancient view before continuing to the top. His kiss promises hope of escaping this decaying fairytale I am bound to. Potent with desire, he watches me undress, his eyes caressing my naked skin.

I let my hair down.

The beating under my ribs quickens, spreading hairline fractures through the bones, cracking open my armour. Pain is my arousal. Marcu undresses and kneels before me. His tongue is a fire in my heat; his fingers explore and enter. I open my mouth, and the valley groans. Marcu reclines and I lower myself onto his waiting body, joining him in rhythm.

An orgasm screams into the valley and returns in echo. A slight tremor ripples through the big red hill. Gripping my hips, he thrusts with passion and lust, writhing in ecstasy, but his climax clouds his senses, blinding him to the heavy rock in my hand that crushes his skull.

I stop. And listen. There is only silence.

A childish giggle escapes into the night; shrieks of a wild fox snatch it away. I lay next to Marcu, embracing his cooling skin, keeping vigil until his bones snap and his teeth rattle as he tumbles down the slope of the big red hill, stopping broken at the bottom. Tomorrow, under a blue sky, the big red hill will feed on his flesh and his blood will quench its thirst. I am alone again, but freedom requires sacrifice and under the next clear moon, I will lay next to Marcu and thank him for this.

Day for Night

Anne Maree Apanski

I feel nothing. Nothing out of the ordinary. I once would have said I had long fingers, but I can see that is not true. Whose hands are these? It has been seventeen days since my last dose and I cling to life with my bony little paws—there are shreds of willpower, like worn-out flag ends flapping in no man's land: storing, photosynthesising, dreaming of rescue, sleeping, sleeping, wake up. Wake up!

I watch the moon cross the sky and stand four ways to every corner of the universe, expanding, breathing, unbounded in darkness. The night is cool and kind now. It never rains anymore; the weather colludes in my dry time. The grasses, brittle and brown, the crickets anxious for some dampness. Think of something nice—*flowers?*

I go outside for the first time in a few days and sit on the veranda, fanning my face with the wind through the trees. This happy moment, to just sit and watch. But nothing happens. The brick house opposite, with its red roof and garden around the brick, stares back. A sickening wave of desperation for IT, the brown sugar, the horse, the 'H' travels my whole body. If I say the word, it will eat me alive.

Aware of single mothers and other desperadoes, I try to comfort myself with the thought that I am not the only person in the world to try to kick a bad habit.

I dream I am in hospital and the doctors are coming to inject us all, to kill us off finally—it is like the end of the war in the camps. Time is against us. We are a drain on resources. I am very weak; I can only find one shoe but hobble to the elevator and step in. The elevator goes down, down, down for miles and opens at the most beautiful dawn I have ever seen, so golden and pink and alive and crisp, and at the bottom is a graphic artist who I know and he waves from the verge where he's having a party and takes my photo. We dig among some rare orchids and find photo albums in which my whole life has been captured. He turns the pages to show me what is there, what has been kept buried and this evokes such sadness, an overwhelming nostalgia for my life and all the people in it.

I dress completely in pink. I am new. I went to the clinic for sleepers and they have a new rap. You *have to* see the nurse first. A young nurse ushers me into an empty office where she pulls out a thick pad of paper and squiggles on it. Perhaps she's mute?

'The pull of addiction is a spiral.' She holds up the pad.

I suppose that is me, the squiggly line on my way to the bottom. I see the twisted worm one inevitably meets with an empty bottle of Tequila.

'I need to sleep, I just want to see the doctor,' I say, trying to cut out all the blather. There is only so much counselling you can take as a long-time addict.

She put me in another waiting room. The kindly Chinese doc is gone—where to? What happens to these old guys? They have a new doctor. A young guy, earnest, full of himself—he's waving his hands in the air like the robot from *Lost in Space*: 'Danger danger, warning warning.' I give up. I set off and borrow ten from a friend. The clinic has gone to the dogs in the short month or so I've been out of the scene.

The phone rings, weirdly—who could be ringing me? It is the employment office. They have two jobs going: photographing buildings for the heritage committee or education officer for the conservation council—right up my alley, they say—a new initiative for creative types to get back to work. I have stood in dole queues for twelve years and never been offered a job. I tell them I am sick and hang up, but the images form: wearing lipstick, dying my hair one shade lighter, smoking Salem instead of Drum, beauticians, friends, rushing, pulling on stockings in the morning, buying flowers in the afternoon, hurrying home with my takeaway, an endless supply of twenty-dollar bills, somewhere to go that isn't the backyard, the bathroom or the shops. This could be my big chance to find out what motivates people. In these organisations, people might have answers and I could be one of them, not a care in the world. What the hell am I waiting for?

I am hired for the conservation job because I can draw and have been to demos. Turns out it *is* right up my alley. My role is to convince farmers and schoolchildren that the environment needs saving and that our National Parks are little conservation zones for the future. Perfect.

First port of call is for the research officer and me to travel south. Get a feel for things.

I pack my ghetto blaster for aural protection and a bag of batteries, and we set off. Zoe prefers to drive. One look at my board shorts and school blazer convinces her that I am not to be trusted. As we drive, she tells me she married her childhood sweetheart and they had come to Australia for his work. They came from New Zealand. All the verbs and nouns in our first conversation are like a foreign language. I put on The Doors and ask her to pull into a bottle shop in the next town. For later, I say, when she gives me the look.

The next town seems practically deserted, except for a few folks tending their shops. We grab some lunch and I remind her again to turn around and go to the bottle shop.

'These people all look dried out, like they've been sandblasted,' I say as she does a uey.

'It's a farming town,' she says.

That doesn't mean anything to me. I guess a farmer would come and get some petrol and food and go home again. I don't understand the quiet emptiness of the drought-ridden paddocks and rusting tin. I need a drink. I don't drink beer, but I doubt swigging wine will go down well, so I insist, at a personal cost to my reputation and possibly my job, that we stop and get a six-pack. She argues with me like she's my wife.

'You're not going to drink it now, are you? While we're driving?'

'Do you want me to drive?'

No, she doesn't want the lunatic in board shorts with a tinnie driving so that is settled. I drink four; we pull over to piss twice. It feels sacrilegious to be drunk in this landscape. Thousands of years before us, humble-quiet, with integrity, the rainbow of greens and yellows and rusts is clear and glinting as if the night can bring the life back, open as the sky and there is me just up off hind legs with this substance abuse problem, pouting at the mountains, wavering before sandalwood and peeing in the long grasses, irreverently plodding and swaying on the waiting earth. She takes photos of me, presumably to prove what an idiot I am either to her husband, who she says will get a laugh out of it, or the boss, who won't. That is enough for me. Anyone getting a laugh is welcome to it.

The trees go for miles, sparse and grim.

'Kilometres,' she corrects me.

'Miles,' I say. 'Don't you prefer the sound of the word? *Milllleessss.*'

She grins, finally cracking up at the kid making fart sounds under her arms. She's no longer afraid of me.

Darkness creeps into spaces between the trees, animals slither and crouch on the ancient footwork, and there is no more music allowed now. It is giving her a headache.

We arrived at O'Connor's place just before six. The driveway is long, providing a great reveal as the house comes into view. Dogs run out from around the house, the sheds, the trees. Mrs O'Connor wipes her hands on her apron and points us in the direction of where to park. Kevin the foster kid and Mr O'Connor emerge from the shed shouting at the dogs so that our introductions can't be heard and I mispronounce Dolly as *Doily*, and then I forget Mr O'Connor's first name within seconds of having heard it.

Dolly has kept the dinner warm and straight away we sit down at the table. It is pork but I am hungry and eat it. Kevin is told off for using his hands to eat sugar from the bowl. I feel anxious. Here, people eat, sleep, and discuss geological formations. Mr O'Connell runs his finger over a map that no doubt would be interesting if you had half a mind. Zoe stands and says she needs to go to bed. Mr O'Connor gets me a beer. Then Zoe tiptoes back past us wearing a long purple nightgown with a giraffe on the front. Mr O'Connor is talking about the folly of the wheat farmers and how they have to diversify and go with nature. He will show us the reforested areas in the morning. I have a vague desire to be adopted and taken care of, like Kevin. I know what it is like to crave and do unscrupulous things.

Neither of us sleeps well as Zoe keeps getting up to go to the kitchen or the toilet. Maybe she has cystitis. Two women sleeping in the same room is supposed to be more fun than this.

We leave early the next morning and I feel that she's tired of me and would rather be at home with her boyfriend.

'Can you turn the music down? I don't like loud music when I'm driving.'

My guess is she doesn't like it anytime. I turn it down but imagine it is loud. Fear is here. The sky watches. I am drying up; I have nothing to offer. I feel like I am four years old being taken by my nan and pop to see their parents out there on the Balonne. The same intermittent stops in dust and silence, night and day. I look out at the sky, at the green that is not England-green but a blur of yellow light and green like mouldy water. Behind the trees along the roadside stretch a thousand miles of stubble and nothing. They had cleared it for wheat. The friendly guardians, the trees—some fierce, some tall and leaning, some old and split—form a guard of honour that seems to acknowledge me as I pass.

Zoe asks if I'm ever going to get married. This is a subject of warmth and safety for her.

'Never,' I say, knowing she's looking for a way to start an inane conversation.

'Laurie and I are going to get married next year if he gets a job in the mines.' She pauses, leading up to her next reveal. 'Do you know what he did the other night?'

'What?'

'He pissed in the wardrobe.'

She pauses again so I understand that I'm expected to drag every mouthful from her.

'Why?'

'I don't know.'

I went back to staring at the trees and listening to Chrissie Hynde on low volume—a miserable vacuum of white noise when paired with the tires on the road at high speed.

The next dried-up turd town lay in squares of baked brown yards sporting one or two grey-barked spindly gums. Flat as death, this town could be named Insomnia because that is surely a likely affliction around these parts.

There is nobody to be seen except for our next host waving us down from her tiny weatherboard, two streets back from the main road. Old Mrs Fox has put off having lunch for two hours until we get there. There are sandwiches, cake and sweet strong tea already under fly covers and doilies. Finally, some warmth seeps towards me.

'I'll just give Coralie Hall a call to come over—she's our researcher.'

She goes into the other room to use the landline and speaks so quietly we can't hear her. She replaces the receiver gently. I have a paranoid moment that I am now in an Australian crime film.

Presently, in walks this short girl with long red hair streaming out from under a pink beanie. She's wearing a 1950s woollen coat that reaches to her knees. A half-suppressed giggle escapes through devilish gaps in her front teeth. I can't wait to get to know her.

Four-wheel drive vehicles arrive one by one, proper troop carriers and old Land Rovers; the entire environmental movement of the south coast seems to be outside beckoning us to follow.

We sit in fear: Coralie, Kevin, me and Zoe, our eyes glued to the car in front of us, the gullies and clay slips, anticipating disaster at any moment.

'In New Zealand ...' Zoe goes on and on about how she's used to these driving conditions.

In our nervousness and exhaustion, the conversation turns to religious experiences.

'I took LSD once,' Coralie says, leaning over the car seat. 'I couldn't talk for six months afterwards.'

'What's LSD?' asks Kevin.

'A treatment for mental illness. You feel things more keenly than normal. Everything seems to make sense,' I tell whoever is listening, suddenly a sage.

Zoe's mouth is pinched shut; she has nothing to add. Kevin gets over-excited and tries to tell the story about the boyfriend's head on a stick. It is a mainstay of teenage culture, one designed to scare the bejesus out of you on a road trip.

I tell them about the time a girlfriend and I were out with two older boys driving up into the hills—we always used to drink and smoke pot up there—and we saw a man as tall as a tree holding his arms out as if he were being crucified and as he stepped out of the darkness his face had no eyes and no mouth.

'He started making these strange clicking noises,' I say, 'like he was trying to communicate or something. We screamed our heads off, jumped in the car, and took off as fast as we could. I've never been so scared.'

Kevin starts screaming. He screams and screams and we try to stop him by screaming louder, this makes it worse so Zoe rouses on us; she has to concentrate on the road.

The sun is long gone. We expect the hikers' cottage to turn up after every bend in the road but it doesn't and, after another hour of fixing our eyes on the backlights of the car in front, we take a turn left.

'This is it!' Kevin yells.

But it isn't—it is another narrower, bumpier track. Twenty minutes later, the oasis of a cabin appears, a sandstone hut on top of a rise. The ranger greets us. Too tired to unpack, we pile in. Others know what to do: light the fire, start the generator for showers and lights, pull out packets of biscuits, salami and cheese. I stand idly smiling until asked to get some extra chairs from outside. As we chomp on our food, the ranger goes over the plan for the weekend. He warns us that the generator must be used sparingly and it is the time of year to see certain flowers.

It is a full moon so after everyone else packs it in Coralie and I take the last of the cask, borrow the torch and go in search of pygmy possums and giant tree-men with no mouths or eyes.

'Look it's the crown-billed thorn-bird.' She points the torch upwards into a spooky dead tree.

'The red-arsed-frilly-tit,' I blurt.

'Here are its tracks!' Coralie is laughing so hard she almost falls over, headfirst.

'Shit, what are those tracks?'

'Kangaroos, you galoot,' she says.

'But those tracks lead back to—us! Run,' I shout, picking up the pace only to trip on a branch that has attached itself to my clothing somehow and felled me hard in the soft, sandy dirt.

Coralie staggers sideways and half falls on me. 'Look at this fucking world, will ya? It's *beeeautiful*.'

We sit down beneath a ridge of ochre, of yellow, pink, red. We breathe in and out and look at each other. We listen to the whispering of night. We don't need the torch; it is bright enough. Coralie passes me the cask and we squeeze out the last guzzle into each other's mouths.

'Did you train as a teacher?' I ask, wondering where such a person comes from.

'No, nothin'. The Commonwealth funded a position the park needed. Best job ever. People are great.'

'Me too. That's how I got my job. Long-term unemployed.'

We stay out there talking like schoolgirls until it gets too cold. Back in our room, we crawl inside our sleeping bags, waking Zoe in the process.

The next morning, I look at Coralie who is sleeping peacefully. She opens her eyes and sees me staring.

'I dreamt of you,' she says.

'What did you dream?'

'I dreamt you were standing beside me and I told you angrily "I really want to flush my guts."'

'That's a good dream, Coralie.'

There is a lot to think about. While everyone else goes on the hike we stay in bed and drink coffee. Before we leave, Zoe refolds my stuff. On the drive back, I look out at the trees and understand what people are doing in these turd towns. They are on the earth, looking after it, or destroying it for wheat. But they love this place.

The moon is shining and full and we keep it in sight on the long drive back to the city. It is my moon. I claim it. And I have a friend, perhaps.

Never Everly

Jocelyn Richardson

A year and a half before Everly gave birth, I asked if she wanted a kid.

She said, 'What if I don't?'

But I knew.

'No, I do,' she said.

There was a twinkle in her eye, as my dad liked to say.

'Back when you were just a twinkle in my eye,' he'd say.

'Ew, Dad,' I'd say.

Ev's partner also had a twinkle. 'Sonia, you're glowing,' I said when I saw her after hearing the news.

'Who me?' Sonia said and we laughed because Ev was already feeling sick. Her teeth ached and her breath was sour. By the time they told me, she was at eight weeks. But I already had my suspicions. Something about the way she clung to Sonia as they arrived at places and entered a room of onlookers. They were both holding onto something. A spiral was tightening.

I had known Sonia for only four years—I couldn't read her as well. Especially since I was still trying to impress her. Older lesbians do that to me. And Sonia was particularly intimidating because she didn't drink. Queer edge, she called it. When the three of us used to go out to crowded bars, she'd be as still as a ship's mast while Ev and I were constantly buffeted. Ev forgot as much of every night as I did, but Sonia remembered everything.

'You don't remember, do you?' she'd say in the morning, bringing us cinnamon buns. Ev and I would inevitably be at the bakery where she worked, watching her move with ease and purpose in her chef clogs and spotless tank top.

'I blame Ev,' I'd say and we all knew that was fair.

Ev was the drink pourer, the wrestler, the booty shaker and one of the messiest people I knew. Her periods shocked her every time and she rarely knew what was going on in the news. She was always off with the literal and figurative fairies. After she and Sonia started dating, she was habitually at bars on Smith Street, not always with me or Sonia. She'd still go after they moved in together, mostly to dance and make out with people. Not with me, obviously. Well, once with me. But I didn't go out nearly as often as she did—I couldn't keep up.

The other giveaways that Ev was pregnant were that she hadn't asked for a tampon and she started checking Twitter.

'Have you been to the Great Barrier Reef?' she asked one day.

It was 2016 and the reefs had just bleached.

'No. Never,' I said.

'Don't use my name in vain,' she said.

She looked out the lounge window of their rental in Coburg and gave a five-minute quiet but impassioned polemic about leopards and anchovies and rates of global warming. 'This year is the warmest since 1880,' she said, which I'd read but never heard anyone say out loud. She sounded drunk, in a good way—heightened—but we weren't drinking because she was several months into the reciprocal IVF program.

When Sonia got home, Ev cried in her arms. 'The coral,' she said and Sonia nodded and kissed her hair. I had a feeling, even then, it was going to happen that day. The world was becoming more real for her.

Eight weeks later, Ev said, 'It took. I'm pregnant.'

We were standing in her hallway with the ceiling light glaring down. I felt exposed, as if I'd been discovered hiding under a table. I saw her shrink into herself. The shell that was Ev housed a new shell. She seemed to be checking on it, swimming with it, and then she returned, Ev, the blushing mother-to-be. Weirdly, I kissed her hand.

'You did it,' I said. 'You're all grown up.'

I have no memory of it, but my mother tells me I asked Ev to be my friend in primary school and she said, 'Maybe'. Her family moved to Altona not long afterwards and she changed schools, so I didn't get to find out if she made a decision either way. Mum thought it was a great joke, which is why, when Ev and I were in the same university Classics class sixteen years later, I was able to piece it back together—our first encounter.

Our tutor prompted us to turn to a partner and recount the origins of our current life ambitions, or in his words, 'The tragedy of our lives'.

Ev and I were sitting next to each other.

'You're Everly Peterson,' I said. 'My mum remembers you.'

We discovered we both lived in the inner north. Her family was still in Altona, near the bay. She used to think she'd become a marine biologist. 'But so did everyone,' she said. 'Because of *Free Willy*.'

My family were still alongside the Monash Freeway, close to the hospital. 'And I nearly became a doctor. Also, I watched a lot of *Grey's Anatomy*.'

We found out we both wanted to be writers—she wanted to be a poet, I wanted to be an investigative journalist. If you'd asked me why, I would have said because I wanted to travel.

But Ev didn't ask. She just gave me her number and apologised for saying 'maybe' when we were six.

'I was a mean kid,' she said, and I was surprised at how ruefully she said it.

'I thought it was a very wise answer, actually. How could you be sure?'

I did travel after university, but not as a journalist. And I didn't write travelogues, but I wrote to Everly. I was on a farmstay in Portugal when she told me she'd met someone, someone older. *She's a pastry chef*, she wrote, *and she handmakes me tiny chocolates in the shape of penguins and vulvas. We fell asleep in the bath together*. It was her first relationship with a woman and for some reason I felt neglectful not being there.

I boasted about staying with a friend of Mum's in Amsterdam. *Had he not been gay I could have perhaps developed a crush on him. He talked with me for hours about everything.*

I gave a hand job to a nice young man called Enes on the night train back to Lisbon, thinking now I would have something to tell her. But I didn't tell her in the end. She might think the whole thing was clichéd, but it wasn't like that and I didn't know how to explain it to her.

When I returned from Portugal, Ev and Sonia picked me up from the airport. Coming out of the terminal, I spotted them behind a bus shelter. They were pressed together. Sonia's head was bowed and Ev's fingers were locked in Sonia's belt loops—forehead to forehead, hip to hip. But there was space between them too.

I often thought of this space when the boys I dated over the next few years were a little clingy. A little close. Patrick. Tyler. Sal. Marc was maybe the worst. I think he wanted a kid with me. But we didn't date long enough to go from condoms to pull-out and, besides, it was around then I went around saying I had a phobia of children. 'I don't understand their minds,' I'd say. 'They're so unpredictable!'

In 2015, I was working as an internal communications coordinator at an office in the city where I maintained HTML and chaired monthly sustainability meetings. Ev, incredibly, was still writing poetry and working on the side doing distribution admin for an artisan tile company. She was starting to get into the production side of things—she'd been out to the kaolin and terracotta quarries in Pittong and was learning to throw pottery, experimenting with glazes. I organised with friends to get her a wheel for her twenty-eighth birthday and a few months later she made me a large hydria-style vase painted with various nudes. 'For holding water, ballot votes or ashes,' she said.

It was the most beautiful object I'd ever owned. When I got it home, I held it around the waist like a dance partner and placed it on the mantelpiece.

Ev explained reciprocal IVF to me as '... putting Fi's bun in my oven'. Then she asked for a loan. 'It's expensive,' she said. 'And I don't want to ask my parents. They might think it means they own half the baby.'

Of course I lent her the money, reminding myself this doesn't mean I own half the baby.

I called my mother around that time. 'You did such a good job with me, relatively. How did you do it?'

'Who says I did?' She paused for effect. 'You told us what to do. In your way.'

'What will happen to Ev?' I asked.

'It changes you. Fundamentally. But Ev will still be Ev. Love ...'

'... doesn't divide. It multiplies,' I finished for her.

'See. You're welcome,' Mum said.

When Ev was heavily pregnant, she wanted to go for long walks on the beach.

'Hi, I'm Everly,' I said when I picked her up. 'I like undinism and long walks on the beach.' Ev taught me that word—a fancy way of saying aroused by water or urine.

We drove forty minutes to the bay and walked for an hour along the bike path. It was late winter by then and blustery. Everyone looked determined to be out in the open.

'But really. You're good?'

She sucked in a breath. 'So happy it hurts.'

On the cliff top, she closed her eyes and a gust of wind rippled over us. She clung to her breasts. 'Ouch ouch ouch. You didn't bring a jacket?'

No, I hadn't brought a jacket.

I threw a tiny stone over the edge and remembered the myth of Penelope from when we were in Classics. 'Her father threw her into the sea when she was a baby. Remember? So his wife wouldn't find out he'd slept with a nymph. But a flock of purple ducks carried her back to the cliff.'

We stared at the gulls hanging in the updrafts.

'Greek myths are so depressing,' Ev said.

I'd never heard her say that. I still found them—not instructive, obviously—but quite moving.

'When are you going to give me names?' I asked.

'Not yet!' she said.

'Even a longlist?'

'It hasn't been easy.' She paused. 'We're thinking Farrah.'

For a moment, I thought it was a reference to the time I layered my fringe and everyone said I looked like Farrah Fawcett.

'It has Irish and Arabic roots. A nod to both sides,' Ev continued.

I nodded. Ev's dad was Irish-Australian. Born in Perth, an Irish town funnily enough. Sonia's mum, Selma, was Lebanese-Australian. It wasn't about me.

'Rah Rah,' I said.

'Farrah,' she repeated.

'Names don't last long,' I said.

'Maybe she can be nameless,' Ev replied. 'So she can be anyone she wants.'

We started back along the bike path the way we came. I thought maybe I'd offended her.

'I'll call her ...' and I zipped my lips.

Ev nodded, satisfied and I hid my relief.

Ev didn't share her poetry with me or anyone anymore. But she'd been published quite a bit back in our university days. One of my favourites had a stanza:

> *To the eternal child,*
>
> *I can't promise you anything.*
>
> *You are new but no better than me.*
>
> *If I could be you, again, again, again!*
>
> *I would be more sensual and less nervous.*
>
> *The rest is for you. This passing trend*
>
> *that window of light*
>
> *this complete lack of repetition.*

In the last month of her pregnancy, I copied it out on a card addressed to the baby-to-be. Ev thought I'd composed it, so I had to explain it was one of hers.

'You remember that?' Ev said.

Her surprise made me think I should've written something of my own. I am an internal communications coordinator.

I sat down at home and it came out: *Welcome, Farrah, to your future. Here, or anywhere you want to go. To be yourself, or anyone you want to be.*

It was a pale comparison. I never shared it.

One evening, a week later, Ev texted, *Now's good*, and I brought frozen dinners and a bag of lettuce over to their house. Farrah, at two days old, was passed to me while Sonia helped Ev take a shower.

Farrah lay in my lap, asleep. Her mouth moved, which meant she was satisfied/dissatisfied? I couldn't tell and I couldn't look away. I regressed through several linguistic stages. In/on, you/me. Me/Farrah, face-to-face.

Ev came back wrapped in a bathrobe and said, 'Hand you the baby and put the kettle in, would I?'

All the fuss they made over her only made me love her more. *She likes this* and *she loves that*. She must be special, I thought, to be so young and know so much about herself.

When I asked about the labour, Sonia said Ev lost a lot of blood. 'Twelve hundred mls,' she clarified, as Farrah let out a gentle cry.

'That does sound like a lot,' I said.

'They gave me an iron infusion,' Ev said, flexing a bicep. She appeared vivid and calm, the way she looked to me after I'd taken one drug or another. All her features were accentuated. Her hair was bigger, her eyes wetter.

In the next moment, I could see she was in pain, though it barely showed. She twirled the belt of her bathrobe and said, 'I'm off to the boudoir.'

I helped Sonia bathe and swaddle Farrah.

'She loves this,' Sonia said and swung Farrah like a pail of water. Her forehead, which had wrinkled as we wrapped her, began to soften.

'She reminds me of myself when I was a baby,' I said. I didn't know how I knew, but it was the only thing that could explain her familiarity.

We crept down the hall and I held the bedroom door open for Sonia. It was dim and hot inside. I averted my eyes when Ev stirred, lifting up a nipple, although I knew she wouldn't mind. I'd seen her boobs before. But she seemed both more vulnerable and more formidable, naked and breastfeeding.

'Goodnight,' I whispered and no one replied.

A few days later, I accidentally smashed Ev's vase that had been holding a dried lotus flower. 'God!' I yelled, feeling an unreasonable amount of despair. As I was cleaning up the shards, Ev texted to see if I wanted to come round to watch the baby while she napped.

When I arrived, Ev was sleeping and Sonia left me with instructions about how to put Farrah in her bassinet.

'No need to look so worried,' she laughed, then left for the shops.

I lay beside Farrah on the rug. 'My head's the size of your body,' I told her. 'I won't be able to say that for long.' She looked at every aspect of my face—my chin, which could just as easily have been my forehead. My mouth, nose. Then she gave her head a little shake and looked away.

When she cried, I began swinging her like I'd seen Sonia do and she draped along my forearm, dozing. That seemed like the right moment, so I took her slowly into Ev's room towards the bassinet. As I leaned over the rail, about to slide her into her sleeping bag, she opened her eyes, expressionless. I couldn't move. I didn't want to frighten her. She might turn against me forever.

Ev had been watching. I was still frozen in place when she laughed and rolled out of bed. In one motion she lifted Farrah out of my arms and into the air. Farrah's face switched like a mask from comic to tragic and back again.

'You don't want her to sleep?' I asked.

'She can sleep in the lounge room.'

In the kitchen, Ev put on some music and poured me a wine, at the same time cradling Farrah in her left arm. Then she lay lengthways along the couch with Farrah in the crook of her torso.

We talked about the old days. The couples who had come and gone. Those who we thought would last but didn't. Those who we thought should break up but didn't because one partner or the other was too controlling or lazy. We talked about my singledom and my options. The fish in the sea.

'There are bigger fish to fry,' I said. 'By which I mean, not fry, but leave in the ocean.'

I noticed Ev wasn't nostalgic. She gave Farrah's stomach a little wobble. 'And here I am, stuck with you,' she joked to Farrah. Then to me, 'Your job is to convince her I'm cool. Don't tell her the bad stuff.'

There was nothing bad I could possibly say.

'And come on,' she said, pressing me. 'There must be someone.'

There was, but, again, how could I possibly say?

'I never told you about the guy I met in Portugal,' I said. 'On a night train. His name was Enes and he offered me candy. It was late at night, past midnight. He said he was from Turkey and started telling me his dad wanted him to be a banker, but he wanted to travel first because he knew how boring banking would be. He said he needed to fit everything good in his life into this one year. I ended up sitting next to him. I made us promise each other we wouldn't get boring when we got older. We shook hands, then lay down together under our jackets on the bench seat. It was slow and muffled. And somehow friendly. We looked into each other's eyes and gave polite little nods, all the way up to his quiet orgasm.'

Ev turned back to Farrah. 'Where is he now?' she asked.

'I don't know.'

'Sounds like maybe you loved him.'

'Maybe,' I said. Then added, 'Well, no.'

'You didn't?'

'I loved you.'

Indira

Anita Thomas

It has been five years since I passed, but my daughter insists on speaking daily. 'Morning Ma,' she begins, cat-stretching beneath the sheets.

She sends fitful thoughts, rat-a-tat questions, apprehensions, observations, some gossip, and caustic humour my way. Lately, though, she seems unmoored. She wants details, wants to make sense of life and death; how we dealt with cancer and dementia as a family. 'We felt powerless,' she says.

I sense introspection.

We never really understood each other even though we loved each other fiercely. We often fought, endlessly and passionately, shoulder to shoulder, nose to nose. Is this a rapprochement, a compulsion for reconciliation?

We should have had these conversations when I was alive, I think, because parsing a life is a long process, and definitely not a neat one; often discombobulating and unpolished. There are transcendent moments, of course. But for her to understand causation and trajectory, I need to start somewhere that makes sense, a point of beginnings. The late 1930s, two decades before I met and fell in love with Antony.

I was born into a Hindu Nair family in a small town in Kerala, India: the seventh girl in a joint family of two brothers married to two sisters; elder to elder, younger to younger, with eight children between them.

You know this, I tell my daughter.

Nairs are a Hindu caste of warriors, a martial nobility, I continue, often compared to the *samurai* of Japan. Our lineage can be traced back to warriors who fought beside Tipu Sultan, the legendary Tiger of Mysore. He was the first Indian ruler to fight the British. Apparently, he was also an ally of Napoleon Bonaparte.

'I now understand where your belligerence comes from,' she replies smoothly. '*Martial nobility* is a good description. You were a tiny pit bull of selfhood, especially when you took the moral high ground. I was proud of you. Fearless and blunt, battling so many issues on so many fronts. Religious prejudice, middle-class snobbery, inquisitive neighbours, grasping relatives. I remember.'

Conflict is probably in our DNA, I reply. Which is not a bad thing; it brings clarity and develops strength of character.

The Nair matrilineal society, in direct contrast to patriliny which reigned everywhere else, had distinct canons circumscribing our lives; marital systems (*sambandham*), matrilineal inheritances (*marumakkathayam*) and joint family structures (*tharavad*), which meant husbands lived in their wife's residences, children took their mother's family name, and women—mothers, sisters, and daughters—inherited the family property.

We Nair women were considered bold and arrogant. Hard to subjugate. Men found it hard to accept our independence.

You should be proud to belong, I say.

We are strong women, I remind her. I want you to know this because it never is easy to be a woman, let alone one who believes in herself.

My father, your grandfather, died before I was ten. Our matrilineal inheritance laws made my mother, my two sisters and myself the sudden legal heirs to half the family property which was considerable enough for my father's older brother *Velliachan* (big father) and his wife *Velliamma* (big mother—my mother's older sister) to become our self-proclaimed parents under the guise of looking after a young widow and her children. It ensured the money and land remained firmly in their control. It fooled no one.

Overnight we—three girls and a boy, not yet teenagers—were no longer 'family'. We were now dependents, vassals, put to work in the fields, sowing, harvesting, reaping, tending crops, weeding the garden, fetching, carrying and cleaning, inside and around the house.

My mother was not spared; she became the housekeeper, childminder to eight, cook, and general factotum. Young, spirited and strong, this independent woman was reduced, overnight, to submission and servitude. She expressed a desire to remarry. Her sister and brother-in-law laid out their conditions: she could remarry as long as she relinquished the custody of us, her four children, and all claims to her share, and our shares, of the property.

'An inspired twofer!' my daughter interjects, caught up in my story. 'Double the wealth *and* free domestic labour. You were just kids! Twice orphaned now.'

It was a painful coming of age, I recall. Neglect, leftovers, hand-me-downs and references to our mother as the slut-whore. We became orphans when she left.

'And your education?' my daughter asks.

As a schoolteacher, Velliachhan could hardly deny us that. We received a rudimentary one, as he thought fit. He even chose our subjects, Sanskrit, Mathematics and Physics.

Our daily routine was a 4 am awakening, a sleepy stumble to a pond some distance from home for a cleansing dip and thence to the temple. Prayers in wet clothes. Flickering lamps, cantillating *pujaris*, bells and chants. *Prasadams*. Rushing home, still damp, to a watery bowl of *kanji*, (rice with its cooking water, your favourite, I remind my daughter) followed by a two- kilometre—or was it three? or four?—long trudge to school.

'Were you barefoot?' she asks. 'Did Velliachhan provide footwear, did the hand-me-downs extend to disintegrating slippers or sandals? I never thought to ask you, Ma, when you told me about your school mornings. I was always impatient with the stories of your childhood—I thought you wanted my pity.'

I did want sympathy; I felt I deserved it. But my daughter didn't understand or care to. Both of us, immersed in and limited by our realities.

Rather unnecessarily, and with typical obduracy (as Velliachhan muttered exasperatedly and repeatedly) I completed school at thirteen, years earlier than I should have. My excuse was I loved studying. I loved knowledge. I wanted to know, and know more.

Further education—for me—was entirely unwarranted, a waste, he decided. *More* money, books and fees. That didn't apply to his daughters, of course, *they* were enrolled in university. Indira should teach, he decided, earn a living and contribute towards food and board.

I hated the idea. I needed to do something drastic. Make my point *unequivocally* so that it never came up ever again.

Confident that no school—not even Velliachhan's—would employ a bald thirteen-year-old, much less as a teacher, I shaved my head. My waist-length hair, my pride and joy, gathered in dense curls around my feet.

'Typical,' mutters my daughter, rolling her eyes. 'No half-measures of course!'

Thwarted and furious, Velliachhan took his revenge, enrolling me in a typing school, the cheapest lucrative option available to discipline a stubborn, hairless teenager. The 'school' was a small room in the home of a kind Brahmin two streets east of our jackfruit grove. I gave no one cause for complaint; I graduated first in the state.

One of Velliachhan's married daughters arrived on a summer visit and possibly appalled by the situation in the family *tharawad*, took me back with her to Calcutta.

'I can't imagine any place more diametrically opposite to your Irinjalakuda of palms, jackfruit, mangoes, rice fields, rivers and boats, *mundus*, long hair and mud paths,' my daughter says. 'That must have been hallucinatory, mind-blowing.'

This was true.

Before Calcutta, I knew nothing of the magic of electricity, of cars and trams. I had never seen rickshaw wallahs yoked like oxen to two-wheeled carriages. All I knew was how to walk across a plank of wood balanced over a well, to walk carefully, using my weight as ballast to draw up pail after pail of water for irrigation.

Calcutta was another world, alien, frightening and exciting. Protests, movements, rallies, meetings, sit-ins and hunger strikes. Partition brought hordes of Bengali Hindu refugees from East Pakistan into the city. Left-leaning parties were in vocal opposition to the Congress government. The literature of Tagore bewitched. I discovered Park Street, patties, sandwiches and pastries, grand pianos and coolies in turbans, tearooms and linens, dinner parties and dancing. It was madness.

I was now living five levels up a dark, winding staircase. Eating daily dinners of *chapati, dal* and potatoes. Studying in a night college for a Bachelor of Arts degree. With a new job as secretary to a Russian in a multinational firm. Wearing saris. Donning dark glasses. Earning my own money, even though I had to hand over each month's salary—in its pristine envelope—to my cousin.

In 1956 I met Antony, a Catholic, on Platform Number 6 of Howrah Station. By design, not chance. He had come hoping for an introduction; he said he had heard about me.

What was I hoping for? I had accompanied my brother on a whim to the railway station; I was free that morning and decided to go along to meet a fellow Irinjalakudan. It was love at first sight. Others might remember it differently. I've heard family stories that Antony lived in an apartment opposite ours, that the balconies faced each other. Above or below? Nobody could recall. The story tells I was slim, feisty and twenty-two. Sleeveless *cholis* and stilettos. Defiant, sassy. Petite, beautiful and oh-so- intelligent. And Antony, a dashing devil-may-care pilot with an exceptional singing voice. Thirty-one, boisterous with song, laughter, and life. Very dramatic! That he serenaded me with popular film songs in Hindi, Malayalam and Tamil, sung tempestuously, and passionately from his balcony in the direction of my bedroom window. That he didn't care who saw or heard. As if it were an Indian version of Romeo and Juliet. He never stood a chance, head over heels in love. And I with him.

'So, different versions', interrupts my daughter. 'What *was* it?'

I ignore her. What does it matter now? It was what it was.

Antony proposed in 1957. Madly in love, we wrote to each other every day of the three hundred and sixty-five days we were engaged.

When we told our families that we were getting married, their reactions were explosive. Speculation ran rife. 'Is she pregnant?' everybody asked, for there could be no other reason for our 'indecent' spurning of protocol, our audacity and our 'lack of respect' for family and elders.

Are you in a situation where you have to marry him? wrote Velliamma in anguish. *Tell me the truth. I beg you, don't do this. Why don't you just kill all of us?*

What did I advise you? A Hindu of any caste or creed is acceptable, but I advised you against marrying a Muslim or a Christian. Do you know how your decision is affecting the rest of the family? Because of what you are doing, an old man, your uncle, will not be able to face his peers or society. He will have to walk with a bowed head.

You—a girl with no parents, no prospects and no future—it will appear that you are being given off to someone. That you were sold for money. People will spit at us! It would have been acceptable if he was a Hindu. But to add insult to injury, a man from Irinjalakuda! And a student of your uncle! How can you be so low-minded?

Both families disinherited us. 'We cannot hold our heads high,' they said. What did they know of love and the intoxicating power of free will?

We fixed a date for our wedding, but Antony did not show up. 'Hah,' snorts my daughter. 'Knowing Dad, he developed cold feet!'

But three weeks later we were wed. Antony flew me to Madras, to a sprawling old house by the highway, a kilometre from the airport, filled with fruit trees: nine varieties of mango, lime, papaya, gooseberry, and drumstick. A laburnum. I remember our cocker spaniel, Goldie, running through the yellow blossoms to our front door, petals drifting in her slipstream.

It was a very old house with no attached bathroom, an outhouse really, some distance away. But you would not remember that, I tell my daughter.

Relatives and extended families of both faiths were unstinting with their prejudices and thinly veiled jealousies. The Catholics were voluble and vitriolic. Hindu censure was thin-lipped derision and pencilled eyebrows raised in supercilious arcs of disapproval.

Antony and I were condemned, banished. And taken advantage of. Relatives came to inspect and assess, presuming familial rights of lodging. What was I like? How did we live? Did I bob my hair?

They came on 'holidays', they came in passing, they sent ill children to be nursed and healed in 'modern' Madras.

I welcomed each one. They *were* family after all.

Weeks into our marriage, I discovered Antony was deeply—and unconcernedly—in debt, a small fact he forgot to mention during our courtship. He earned four hundred and thirty-two rupees a month as a newly minted airline pilot; he had to pay back a loan of twenty-five thousand.

Years into our marriage, I discovered his serial infidelities. I opened a bottle of his treasured whisky, made a bonfire of our letters, and watched love incinerate as I drank myself into a short oblivion. I never touched alcohol again.

Betrayal is cataclysmic. It is anguish, despair, anger, unfathomable pain. But you have no choice, you cannot succumb to it, you have to bear it and bear it alone. Life has to go on. I had three children and no family support of any kind. It gave me focus and perspective; everything else became inconsequential in the determination to survive with my head held high. The first tenet of my personal philosophy evolved: never look back.

My daughter only remembers that I became suffocatingly self-righteous, pious even, in my thirties. 'Worse than my mother-in-law,' she grins, hoping for a retort that gives more away. I resist. For now anyway.

What does *she* know? This is a long story; I am just beginning.

Kerania versus the Dream

Vicki Kyriakakis

I

Kerania Diakara looks out over the blustering sea and thinks about the fish. Her son stands like a stocky Odysseus on the bow of his ship *The Penelope*, gazing out over the Eloundian bay. He's yelling out orders the way he yells for food—too loudly and with no tact. He's overseeing preparations for the Eloundian boats to join the fight against the Ottomans, to push the invader out. It's not him she's focused on, however, as he stands there with his hands on his hips. Kerania thinks instead about the red mullet, swimming unspoiled beneath the hulls of the moored Cretan boats. It could be swimming in olive oil instead, with a bit of garlic and lemon, to be fried up for dinner, if only Apostolos had thought to take care of this one thing before he left. If only he'd thought of his mother at all.

It's Captain Apostolos now though, she supposes, and she can't help the stab of pride despite her fury about the mullet. Her spine straightens so she looks taller than her five-foot-two-inch frame. Mothers and wives and daughters stand alongside her on the shore in a line of feminine obedience. Despite her height, she is the tallest of them, she thinks.

She feels something else there too, darker and wilder. Something lower in her groin and hidden under her skirts, something she thought long ago destroyed.

The Dream.

It crawls out from its hiding place and, with a twitch of its bat-like wrist, deposits her on the stern of *The Penelope*. It slings a *toufeki* low across her waist threading wind through her hair, tossing her son onto the shore and emptying his larder. The Dream gives her pleated breeches and makes her son wear a stifling skirt, adorning her head with a fringed kerchief, his with a widow's scarf. She would do a better job of command, the Dream whispers. They'd have been sailing hours ago. They wouldn't be in danger of missing the Cretan fleet near Heraklion. They'd be first among the brave.

If she had been born with balls between her legs, hung low like her husband's, she could have torn the beating heart from an Ottoman chest, the Dream whispers. If she were a man, she might have plucked a winsome beauty off a roof on Kasos and sucked protest from her lips. She'd have wooed gently, the Dream insists.

Kerania breathes in and exhaling, shoves the Dream back under her skirts. She knows how to bury things. Her people have been burying things for thousands of years. Since Arkadi, and the innocents slain there, they've buried dreams. Since Egyptian mercenaries joined the Ottomans to slaughter hundreds of her fellow Kasiots on the island of her birth. Since Constantinople fell. Since Megas Alexandros rode across the Steppes leaving his people behind. Since the Gods on Olympus sent firestorms to destroy the bloodline of King Minos.

A Dream like this one? That's the easiest thing to be rid of. It's not a husband, unwanted but needed, sent to his grave with too much *tsipouro*. It's not a mother, dead from the grief of never again seeing her daughter. It's not a son leaving his mother behind.

The Dream clings to Kerania's legs as her widow's scarf flaps against the Cretan wind and her pepper-coloured hair whips across her face. It tries to claw its way back up with nails that bite. On board *The Penelope*, Apostolos urges the men to move faster. They are little more than an army of merchant boats made war-ready with spit and a prayer. There are twenty in total, a big number for a small village. The boats bounce in the choppy waters as the ropes are tied, and the sails hoisted. Men rush from one to the other, climbing down ladders and up planks, scrambling to make them ready. Dark hair is plastered against sweaty foreheads. Kerania watches them until the last boat has left the harbour and her son has vanished from her sight. She watches and curses the Ottomans, and the sea, and the space between her legs.

Kerania watches and presses her hand down hard upon the head of the Dream and thinks stubbornly of the mullet.

II

The church Kerania is baptised in is barely three metres in each direction. It's lit by hundreds of half-melted candles stuck in rows of sand-filled trays. It's perched at the end of a craggy pass, reachable only via a path that winds up steps hewn from rock. On the day of her baptism at two years old, so the story goes, her mother had to carry her up on her back through the heat and dust, bent over like a mule muttering prayers and curses. Kerania's father wasn't there, having died the year before with five hundred other men who'd been slaughtered by the invaders. It was left to her mother to ensure the child didn't fall to Satan. Hers had been a difficult birth, with lots of blood. Her aunts would daily remind her how much trouble she'd caused, coming into the world back-to-front like a stubborn donkey. It was mothers' blood that couldn't be spared given how much had already been spilled on Kasos, they said. As an only child and a girl, she had to pay it back with her obedience, since a dowry was something she would never be gifted and men were hard to come by.

Kerania tells herself she doesn't care. At sixteen, she sits on the roof of their whitewashed house and sucks on the lemons she picks from their tree, ignoring the yells of the matriarch below. The lemons match her soul—tangy and sharp and not altogether edible. She spits the pips out like her mother spits at her to ward off the evil eye.

From this vantage point, she can just see over the trees to the edge of the sea. The few Kasiot boats left after the massacre are tied like chastened slaves. She hates the look of them, thinks often of going down there and cutting them free, but her mother assures Kerania that such a thing would kill her with shame and Kerania is not so heartless as to wish her mother dead. Her eyes stray to the boats often and her mind strays further and her heart further still and it's while contemplating the boats and sucking on the flesh of a particularly ripe lemon that Kerania first becomes aware of the Dream.

It is hairy and thin, pasty from lack of light. Its teeth are sharp. Its eyes are round and bright. Its bat-like wings are folded tight against its back. It settles beside her on the roof and points one thin claw towards the melting sun and squeals with delight.

Kerania is startled out of her reverie. This is a new thing, this wild excitement, this heart-pounding sense of something more. How long has the Dream been there? Why didn't it say something before now?

The Dream whispers it has been here since the day of her birth. Oh, it didn't arrive the way she did, screaming like a Fury and covered in slime. It arrived piece by piece in the still of night, whispered longing laying flesh across its bones, every desperate passion a threaded vein. Now it's strong enough to be seen and it wants to talk.

About what? Kerania asks, staring at the sunset.

About everything, the Dream breathes.

III

Kerania and the Dream sit often on the roof, walk along the rocky shoreline and hang upside down together from the lemon tree, letting their hair dangle against the ground. In the deep night, the Dream places its face near hers and shows Kerania things from other worlds. In the day, Kerania sits arm in arm with it by the front door waiting for something only the Dream can see. The Dream holds her close and caresses her cheek and kisses her eyelids. Kerania's mother and aunts yell at her more than before, now that the Dream is here, but the Dream covers Kerania's ears with its bat-like hands and muffles their voices. It softens her pillow at night and fills her dreams with visions of the mighty Oceanos, of the dreaded Charybdis and songs of the Sirens, of the grey-eyed Athena and her mighty shield. In the morning it beckons her into the hills where butterflies brush her skin and jasmine tickles her nose and the *Anemoi* sigh with longings that thrill her.

Kerania and the Dream become inseparable. The Dream is the only warmth she needs and in return she feeds the Dream the passion it requires.

Could I run through the woods like Artemis? Kerania asks the Dream. *Could I stand on the tallest mountain in Greece and sing to the gods? Could I stretch my arms out, and launch off the cliff tops and fly? Could I dance with the stars?*

Yes, the Dream assures her. *You could do that. You can do anything.*

IV

He is a stocky man with a full moustache, bandied legs and hard shoulders. His arms are longer than they should be, but his chest is all *palikari*, her mother says. He is a laddish clump of clay come to bestow worth on Kerania with his attention. His laugh is big, his presence bigger. The women in the house make space for him like water rushing away from an oil spill. They race to make him *kafe* and bring him a slice of *bougatsa* as he surveys his kingdom from their doorway. When he appears, Mihalis Zervandonakis takes up the whole of their world. He blocks out the sun.

'I have a boat,' Mihalis brags to them. 'I sailed from Aghios with it. I carved it myself. I mend the nets the fish get trapped in. I catch many fish and make a lot of money. I have good, strong hands.'

He lays out his palms for Kerania. 'You like strong hands?' He winks.

Kerania blushes, but not from modesty. Rather it's from the hot swell of rage that pops in her gut, spreading through her veins. There is no reason that she can find for her reaction—she doesn't understand what it means or why her mother's face turns pink. It just feels in-her-bones-wrong, and the Dream agrees for it pulls her sharply towards the room she sleeps in with her aunt and away from him. She flees the raucous laughter that follows like she's fleeing the Fates themselves.

V

The wedding is small and over quickly. They hold it forty days later in the same church Kerania was baptised in and with the same priest. She wears the lace dress her mother was married in, and her grandmother before that, although it gapes at her waist and has been too-much mended. Their wedding *stefana* are created using the wildflowers that grow on the steps beside the church. Her aunts weave them together while singing folk songs that are half celebration, half dirge. Mihalis does not even trim his moustache for the occasion. He keeps it full and hairy. Kerania stares at it the entire time, avoiding Mihalis' eyes while she repeats the priest's words. Her brain processes half of what is said.

The night that follows is painful. She has only just begun exploring herself down there, understanding the ebbs and folds of her changing body, what draws pleasure and what indifference and what pain. She has only just discovered there was something there to find. Now it belongs to Mihalis, and he has less knowledge of her body than she does and none of the interest in unfolding its secrets. He is like the Minotaur tearing through the labyrinth, like Jason stealing the Golden Fleece. Afterwards, she folds in on herself and draws as far from him as her mother's bed and his snoring will allow. She draws the Dream out from its corner and asks: *Is this the thing you saw coming? Why doesn't it feel any good?* But the Dream is silent. It blinks at her with bat-like eyes. Kerania feels its thoughts collide with her own, all of them miserable.

The day she departs Kasos for good, she sees relief battling with grief in her mother's eyes. 'The world is hard for women without men, Kerania,' her mother says. 'Just ask your aunts. Mihalis asked for no dowry. You'll be taken care of.' They are the only words her mother will gift her to explain the sudden upending of Kerania's world. They are the last words they will say to each other this side of life.

The Dream still does not dare speak. The Dream is thinking and watching. The Dream cannot explain the strange turn that has appeared in the road it had mapped out for them both.

VI

Slowly, but without noticing, the air between Kerania and The Dream grows cold. It still whispers to her as she's transported like Ariadne across the Aegean sea, deposited in Aghios Nikolaos with all the tenderness of a betraying Theseus. It mutters as she is left behind to find her own way in a new town and home, while Mihalis sails away again and again for adventures and loves she will never enjoy. It hisses when she tries to do all the things her mother did for so long, things she developed no taste for. But every day is like the next here. There are no trees to hang from, no roofs she's allowed to sit on. The horizon is a world away. Her belly swells with the first of several miscarriages before she finally gives birth in a tidal wave of pain and relief to a baby boy. The Dream's ambitions grow muted. It talks no longer of songs that could catch the ears of the gods. It whispers instead of the tablecloth she might ask Mihalis to buy, or the harbour view she might take in. It reminds her of the song she might sing when she is alone or of the release to be found between her legs while Mihalis sleeps. When her son is born, it speaks of dreams for him and what he might become. At first, she listens and some of these small dreams come true, but many do not and Kerania learns to mistrust the Dream, resenting it. Kerania asks it questions it cannot answer and demands to know why it came to her at all, since it proved so untrustworthy. The Dream in turn becomes hairier, like some sick thing writhing in her belly. There comes a time when they no longer talk at all, though the Dream is ever fretful at the periphery of her vision and its promises never closer than the nearest star.

VII

Without the red mullet, Kerania is forced to rely on a handful of small olives and hard, crusty bread for her dinner. She pairs it with the last of the *kefalograviera* she has from Apostolos' send-off and calls her empty stomach filled. Her son will send more money, but it won't arrive for days. For now, Kerania cuts the last lemon and pops a small slice in her mouth. The zestiness explodes across her tongue. For a second it smooths the skin around her eyes. It darkens her hair. The Dream stirs beneath her skirts. Then the taste passes, and she is old again, her joints aching, and her legs stiff. She tuts and throws the rest of the lemon away.

'That's life,' she mutters.

The Dream bristles.

You don't need to be here, she growls at it. *Who told you that you had to stay?*

The Dream goes quiet, but it doesn't leave.

VIII

Kerania dies on a Sunday. Her son is there with his wife and her grandson. Neighbours come to say goodbye. The priest reads the last rites and sprinkles water across her face. It has been a good life they tell her. She gave birth to a leader in the community. She has a grandson of whom she can be proud. She has done her duty. There is nothing more for her to do, no more is needed. By any measure of a woman, her life has been a success.

Kerania hears none of them. She waits for them to leave until it is just her in the fading twilight. When everyone else has gone to sleep, the Dream finally slinks out of its corner and draws near to her for the first time in years. It lies down next to her, its face close to hers, their hair mingling like days of old. It folds a bat-like hand over her cold one and rests its temple against hers.

Many years from now, it whispers, *in another place and time, there is a dark-haired girl-child that has fire for veins and stars for eyes. She has your strength and will. She has your intelligence. She has your stubborn pride. She is like you in so many ways. She likes lemons and odd jokes. Her soul sparkles. She is a match for any man. She can move mountains. And I promise you, she will sing to the gods. She will run through forests with the wind in her hair. She will commune with the trees. She will dance with the stars and kiss any lips she fancies. She will do everything you didn't get a chance to do. And she will know your name Kerania Diakara, this I promise.*

The Dream kisses her temple. It smooths her furrowed brow. Kerania smiles, sighs. Only then does the Dream spread its great bat-like wings and fly away.

Cubicle

Dean Kerrison

Negar and I are inside a café in Iran's capital, Tehran. She says her English isn't great. But it's good enough. Her eyes are unrealistically blue—not like the sea but an Avatar's skin. Contact lenses.

She's doing her master's and teaches Persian to speakers of other languages. I try finding out what she likes to do in her spare time. Nothing except sleep. Boring.

My iced latte and her virgin mojito take almost fifteen minutes for some reason. Older men are smoking but the strong air conditioning somewhat neutralises the fumes.

After my suggestion of going to the park, Negar says we should take a taxi.

Google Maps is open on her phone.

'Why?' I ask. 'It's just up the road.'

'It looks near but it's further than it seems.'

I press the walking directions icon in the app. 'Are you serious? It's only four hundred metres, seven minutes by foot. Let's walk. Don't be lazy.'

Holding hands at Laleh Park, we pass people sitting on shady benches, cats curling up in the dirt, trimmed hedges lining a water feature. We sit under an enormous sycamore tree, partly concealing ourselves behind the fat trunk. I close my eyes and listen. Flowing fountain, high-pitched chirping, children at a distant playground. Negar and I make out. My hand lies on her waist, circles beneath her shirt, finds her hardening nipple. We take a break.

'I'd like to lie down,' she says.

'You're sleepy?'

'Yes, a little. But it's not good for women to lie down here.'

I lie on the grass next to her anyway, my hand feeling her thigh over her jeans while she sits. Her hand slides under my pants and starts rubbing me. A man walks past, dressed in some kind of maintenance uniform. Shit. Negar takes her hand off me. The man looks back over his shoulder and says something in Persian.

'He says there's police around.'

Through the winding path, we move towards the bathrooms. After I'm finished, I wait for Negar outside the women's. She exits and we walk to the front of the men's.

'Let's go in together,' I say.

'Are you sure? I think there's cameras.'

'I've looked already. No cameras.'

'Okay, quick.'

Six cubicles line one edge and another five run across. We enter the larger one designed for special needs. I lock the door. Our hands all over each other. Mint residue from her drink on my tongue. Pants below our knees. My left fingers inside her. Right hand covering her mouth when she moans.

'You have protection?'

I put on a condom, guide her hips to turn and face the wall. After five minutes I hear a sudden metallic scraping. And footsteps. Someone opens a bathroom door, the one at the end. It's not a person using the toilet. Objects bump each other lightly. It's a cleaner for sure. He's mopping the floor now while Negar's getting wetter. We're fucking more quietly. Kissing her neck, wondering how we're supposed to get out of here unseen, I see the tension in her squeezed lips, trapped expression. One last thrust. I hold in my sigh and pull out. Without making a sound, I carefully tie a knot on the condom, wrap it in a tissue, as Negar silently pulls up her jeans and adjusts her hijab.

The cleaner is in the second cubicle. If we wait, he's not gonna leave before us. He'll try to open our door sooner or later. On my phone I type: 'I'll head out first and walk out to the right-hand side. You follow after.'

I walk out and see the man mopping the cubicle floor, but he doesn't look up at me.

In the park I wait. Thirty long seconds. A minute. Too anxious to sit still. Pacing around. Two more damn minutes. What's going on? She's out. Looking tense, facing the ground, she sees my waving. When she reaches me, she's in tears and sits on a bench.

'What happened? What kept you?'

'The two men wouldn't let me out.'

'Two? What do you mean? I only saw one and he didn't see me.'

She tries to reply but her sobs swallow the words.

'Let's get out of this place first,' I continue. 'Tell me on the way.' I almost hold her hand before wondering if even that action might draw attention our way.

Passing palm trees and pink-flowered shrubs along the concrete pathway, she calms down somewhat.

'They asked what I was doing in there. I said I thought it was the women's bathroom and made a mistake. The man said he saw you, knew you're not my boyfriend and why was I doing this with you. He said he should call the police.'

I grab her hand and walk faster. 'Then what did you say?'

'I started crying and admitted and promised not to do it again.'

'Did they take your name or anything?'

'They said they should. But they let me go.'

Inside the metro station, we head in the same direction. Metro trains anywhere in Iran have two sections: mixed-sex carriages and a female-only one. At the platform, a dozen women wait at one end, while a fairly equal assortment of both sexes line the remainder across the marble diamond tiles. Loud, relaxed chatter echoes. Negar stays with me in front of the mixed section.

I follow her aboard the full train. Many people are talking inside. We stand at a pole.

'This was dangerous,' she says.

'Yeah, I know. A bit too dangerous.' Before reaching her stop, I ask what would have happened if the men called the police.

'We would've been locked up for a night or two.'

I'm overly cautious not to touch her at all.

'Here's my stop,' she says.

We shake hands like business partners after a buffet lunch. Negar disembarks, turns back around after a few steps, her half-smile receding behind the flock between us and, as the train speeds along, I ignore a merchant in the aisle selling mobile chargers and accessories, yelling his sales spiel in Persian mixed with the English words 'Android' and 'power bank', but while my gaze holds through a blurry window, there's nothing amid the bleak tunnel, just a void filled by shouts of dissonance layered with more empty space.

Orang Bati

Tika Widya

Malika stormed out of the village head's house. She slammed the door in Ahver's face, shouting, *'Kamorang panggil lagi saya setelah lulus sakola!'*[1] She no longer heard Ahver's answer. Malika struggled to hold back her anger. She took a deep breath before turning and walking to where her daughter was waiting for her.

As Malika approached, Kinara was looking at the pebbles at her feet. Malika could feel the uneasiness in her daughter's heart. Her daughter resembled the look of water. The stream was swift on the inside but calm on the outside. Raising Kinara for thirteen years had ensured the love between them existed beyond time and space. They nodded at each other, knowing this was no safe place for a conversation. Slowly, they walked back to their tiny hut on the hill.

Malika opened the door of their hut, which was like an oasis in the desert for the two of them. *'Ose taru akang di situ dolo?'*[2] Malika

---

1   Kamorang panggil lagi saya setelah lulus sakola = you call me again after graduating school!
2   Ose taru akang di situ dolo = you put it there first.

asked her daughter to put down the *amanisal*[3] on the kitchen table. Malika prepared water in the loo. 'Take a shower first,' she said.

Kinara stepped forward. 'The water isn't cold, is it?'

Malika shook her head. Coastal waters were never cold.

Not long after, Kinara was already soaking in a wooden bucket that looked too small for her tall body. Malika was washing her daughter's face, which was covered in mud, when Kinara asked, 'Mama, am I troublesome?'

Malika examined her daughter's face which, as usual, resembled the appearance of calm water. 'No.' As far as Malika could remember, Kinara was the only thing that made her life blissful.

'Mama, aren't you afraid of me?' Kinara asked while trying to reach her back.

Malika helped her daughter scrub herself. Kinara was born with a large lump on her back that made her look nothing like a normal thirteen-year-old. She had to walk hunched over with the lump growing bigger every year. The village shaman said it was a curse. The curse that was cast upon Malika, who fell pregnant out of wedlock. Kinara was born without a father.

'Why should I be afraid of *ose*?'[4] Malika replied.

Kinara peered down silently. Malika suspected Kinara was searching for the right words. Kinara looked into her mother's eyes and said, '*Dorang*[5] told me that I'm *Orang Bati*[6] who eats all their cattle. That's why they throw mud at *beta*.'

---

3 Amanisal = fish basket.
4 Ose = you.
5 Dorang = they.
6 Orang Bati or Bati people are mystical creatures with bat wings and are believed to like eating human babies. Bati people are not the same as Bati ethnic (community).

Malika stopped scrubbing wounds and bruises. She smiled. 'I don't see you had any wings like *Orang Bati*.'

'And I'm definitely not eating babies, Mama,' Kinara said.

They laughed. It was not the first time they had faced a challenge together. For years, Malika and Kinara had been treated like second-class villagers. They were often accused of things they'd never done. Malika was detested because the people believed Malika's father was a vile shaman. Kinara was despised because people had never accepted the disabled child. Perhaps, a remote island with a population of no more than a hundred people had always been suspicious of anyone different.

'Kinara, a good sailor, was never born out of a calm sea. I know it's not easy, but Mama still loves *Ose*. *Ose* are my only child.' Malika brushed Kinara's wet hair and got up to get a towel.

'Mama is also the only one for *beta*[7], since *beta* has no father.'

Malika's throat was clogged. Her daughter's words had taken their toll for quite a while. Kinara stood up in the bucket and finally took the towel herself. This made Malika snap out of her thoughts and start their dinner. The two ate fish soup while laughing a lot.

Evening greeted them with a purplish sky hanging over their islet. Suddenly, there was a knock on the tiny cottage door.

'Malika, *betong*[8] need to talk.'

Malika heard the voice of Ahver, the village leader, coming from outside the hut. Her face stiffened. She opened the door to find dozens of villagers carrying torches. Malika clenched her fists.

'What else do you want?' Ahver wiped the sweat from his forehead. '*Beta* can no longer stop them.'

---

7   Beta = me or I.
8   Betong = we.

Malika looked like she was about to pounce on Ahver.

'Hold your tongue, drag *dorang badua*[9] now!' A ruthless voice emerged from the crowd commanding Malika. She recognised the voice and quickly spotted the man who had pushed through the throng of villagers.

'What else would *ose* take from me, Bora?' Malika screamed.

Before Malika could attack Bora, several other men swiftly ambushed and silenced her. Not only did they drag Kinara out of the house, but they also held down Malika. She struggled, but it was an unfair match.

The villagers took Malika and Kinara to Tebing Tinggi[10]. This place was so named because it was the highest cliff on their small island and directly overlooked the open sea. The waves crashing against the rocks sounded like thunder. The sky was no longer purple. Malika immediately realised what they wanted. Fear clung to her along with the arrival of dark clouds. She struggled even more and finally they let her go.

'Release *ana parampuang beta!*'[11] Malika vented her anger at once. A machete was then placed at Kinara's neck. '*Katong*[12] wouldn't want to go through this trouble if it weren't for the interests of the village,' Bora said.

Ahver, the village head, came running behind Bora. 'Ua[13] Maria's baby dies, Malika!'

---

9 Dorang badua = both of them.
10 Tebing Tinggi = high cliff.
11 Ana parampuang beta = my daughter.
12 Katong = our people.
13 Ua = aunt.

Malika shook her head. 'It has nothing to do with *beta* and Kinara!' Bora stood between Malika and Ahver. He then put the tip of his machete beneath Malika's chin. '*Ose* talk too much!' he grunted.

Malika spat on Bora's face.

The man raised his machete as Ahver shouted, 'Enough!'

More and more people came to Tebing Tinggil. The sound of their marching rumbled through the air. Malika could hear many of them demanding a verdict for her daughter. They accused Kinara of being the sole cause of the death of Ua Maria's baby. *Orang Bati*—that's how they whispered the name of Malika's daughter. They believed that Kinara was an evil-winged creature that ate babies. When no one else came, Ahver stopped the crowd's buzz by inviting them to pray.

'Hilarious!' Malika snapped. 'You dragged *ana beta*[14] to the cliff to pray! What do you expect? For a demon to come out of her body?'

Bora ambushed Malika from behind and covered her mouth with his palm. '*Ose* asked for this, Malika!' Bora whispered in her ear.

Malika winced in disgust when she felt something harden behind her.

'As you have heard, it's true, Ua Maria's baby who was born today died shortly after touching the ground of this island,' Ahver said.

Some villagers appeared dazed. Some muttered to each other while pointing at Kinara. Malika glanced at her daughter with growing concern. Fear spread through her body as fast as lightning.

'Never once has this happened before,' Ahver declared. '*Beta* understood your concern. 'When strange things happen, then

---

14 Ana beta = my child.

katong as the successor to the island shall immediately deal with it, no matter what!'

Ahver was applauded by the villagers. Malika struggled to free herself but Bora was too strong.

Ahver approached Kinara. Before Ahver opened his mouth, she asked, 'If *beta* obeys, will *ose* let Mama go?'

Malika struggled once again when she heard these words, but it was still useless. Ahver nodded slowly. Malika saw her daughter throw Ahver a sharp look. The girl seemed to be contemplating whether the other person could be trusted.

Her gaze softened for a split second, but then Ahver turned and whispered something else in her ear. Malika tried hard to hear, but every word was crushed by the rushing waves and the people's clamour. Ahver finally asked the villagers to release Kinara.

Malika breathed a sigh of relief. Fear transformed into something warm in her chest. Perhaps they would all wake from this madness and set her daughter free. Mercifully, she took another deep breath. The storm might have been over.

However, reality struck like blistering thunder. Without warning, Kinara gave Malika a faint smile then ran and jumped off the cliff. At first, Malika did not understand what was happening, but a second later realisation stabbed like a dagger. Bora released Malika who then ran to the edge of the cliff and wailed for her only child. The waves continued to crash and the sky began to rumble with pending rain. Malika's screech united with nature's commotion.

Ahver approached Malika and she felt the touch of his hand on her shoulder. Sadness turned into anger and a desire for revenge. Malika ran towards Bora who managed to snatch Bora's machete from its scabbard. She swung the machete while crying and laughing, and Bora retreated.

'Malika ...' Ahver tried to calm her down.

Malika pointed the machete at Ahver's neck, who then raised his hand.

'Shut up!' she screamed. 'Just close your eyes like you did fourteen years ago.' Malika's dead stare shot like a bullet through Ahver's head. The villagers did not dare to approach—their village leader's life was at stake. 'Tell them what those people did to *beta*!' Malika pressed the machete against Ahver's skin.

'Malika, I once was nobody,' Ahver said. 'Now things are different.'

'If it's true that things have changed. Why weren't you dragged by the five men to Tebing Tinggi?' Malika asked. Before Ahver could answer, Malika gave an odd laugh. 'Without a doubt, *parampuang*[15], Kinara and I are clearly not worthy of your protection. *You* saw Bora and his friends molest me, but *you* say nothing. Why aren't their heads rolling? Why does it have to be *ana parampuang beta*[16]? Do you know what kind of hell I've been through ever since?' Malika's tears mixed with the rain that had begun to fall. She recalled how shocked and scared she'd been when she found out she was pregnant due to the pillage of those monsters. It had been brutal. But she also remembered how her efforts to hate had melted away when she first held Kinara.

Malika laughed—maybe it was her fate to live in this isolated way. It was she who had brought bad luck to Kinara. Her daughter was a victim of unresolved injustice. Malika turned to the crowd of villagers who had fallen silent. Bora and his friends were gone, nowhere to

---

15 Parampuang = woman.

16 Ana parampuang beta = my daughter.

be seen. Even if they had stayed, Malika wasn't sure she could fight them. Her helplessness had quashed the prospect of revenge.

Ahver fell to his knees. 'Forgive me, Malika!'

Rage choked her again as she slashed her way towards Ahver. Still, she was only able to make a scratch on Ahver's cheek. Malika laughed once more at her helplessness. What else was there to do? 'Ahver,' she whispered, 'a coward like *ose* may live longer indeed.' Without thinking, Malika ran and jumped from the cliff, following her daughter's footsteps.

In silence, she enjoyed the remaining seconds of her life. Malika had just flashed a parting smile to the world when something grabbed her shoulder and stopped her from falling. She looked up to see a pair of bat wings flapping gently. Malika gasped. She recognised that face—her daughter was alive. Kinara had saved her. The lump on Kinara's back had turned into a pair of wings—her daughter truly was the *Orang Bati*.

Kinara brought Malika back to the top of Tebing Tinggi. Malika was willing to bet that several people from the crowd of villagers must have fainted witnessing all of this. Ahver ran as if he knew what was about to happen—he had dug his own grave.

Kinara landed Malika slowly. 'Mama, a strong sailor is never born out of a calm sea.'

Malika nodded tearfully.

Kinara asked her mother to close her eyes. Malika agreed. Soon after, Malika heard people screaming. She chuckled as she smelled the rotten scent of blood. Revenge could never have tasted sweeter.

Biographies

Anne Maree Apanski has been published in *Pub Fiction*, Allen & Unwin, and *Warp Drive*, Random House, *Baby Teeth* collective and had work performed with Spineless Wonders at the Sydney Writers Festival. Influenced by Solzhenitsyn and Carver, she is currently working on a novel lampooning the immigration department.

Catherine Armitage is a writer and editor based on the Wangal lands of the Eora nation. She was formerly an editor for the scientific journal *Nature*, a senior writer for the *Sydney Morning Herald*, and a China correspondent and Higher Education Editor for *The Australian*. With a Master's Degree in Creative Writing from the University of Technology, Sydney, she now writes fiction full-time and is working on her first novel, a story of possession and dispossession set in rural New South Wales where she grew up. Her story 'The True Light of Day is Constant' won the 2022 Australasian Association of Writing Programs/ASSF Emerging Writers' Prize.

Ruth Armstrong has worked as a doctor, a medical journal editor and a public health writer/blogger. Based on Gadigal and Wangal land in Sydney for many years, she is most at home in the ocean (any ocean). She has an MA in creative writing from the University of Technology Sydney. The winner of the 2018 AAWP/ASSF Emerging Writers' Prize and the 2022 Olga Masters Short Story Award, her short stories have been published in *Meniscus*, *Island Magazine* and the *ACE* and *UTS* anthologies.

Joshua Baird writes from unceded Wadawurrung Country. His short fiction, nonfiction, and poetry have been published in various Australian journals and he is the 2020 recipient of the Matthew Rocca Poetry Prize. He has a PhD in Creative Writing and teaches at Deakin and Swinburne universities. His work often explores links between masculinity and unreliable narration.

Josephine Browne writes on unceded Bundjalung Country about human-animal relationships and masculinities. Her writing has appeared in a range of publications, including *Hecate*, *Overland*, *Island* and *TEXT Journal*. Her co-edited collection on human-animal relations, pandemic and climate crises is contracted with Routledge. She was short-listed for the Peter Carey Short Story Award 2023, and the story appearing in this Anthology, 'Ewe', is part of a forthcoming collection co-written with Chantelle Bayes. Josephine is currently a Narrative Therapist and sociologist at Southern Cross University.

Bec Curtin is a teacher and former journalist who loves to tell a good yarn. She is a passionate storyteller, particularly about dysfunctional

Australian families. In 2022 she won the Maureen Freer Literary Competition and was shortlisted in the Sydney Hammond Short Story Award.

Jake Dean writes stories and rides waves on Kaurna Country in South Australia. His fiction has been recognised in journals, anthologies and contests across Australia and abroad. He lives alongside a nude beach with his wife, two sons and kelpies. You can read more of his work at jake-dean.com.

Andrew Drummond's writing has appeared in *Meniscus*, *Explore*, *juice*, *Rabelais*, *ars poetica* and a number of anthologies. He was the winner of the 2017 Australasian Association of Writing Programs/ Ubud Writers & Readers Festival Emerging Writers' Prize.

Rafael E. Fajer Camus is a Mexican writer who was educated at NYU and Naropa University. He has travelled extensively and has lived in Mexico City, Paris, and NYC. He's been through a few rehab treatments in the US and Mexico. He's also spent time in psychiatric treatment centres. He's now aware that he's not a cyborg destined to settle humans on Mars and is working on his first book *Notes on the Borderline* from which his story 'COVIDIOT' is excerpted.

Sarah Giles (she/her) is a writer and PhD candidate at Swinburne University. She is researching the possibilities of the contemporary short story cycle as a means for exploring women's experiences of isolation, trauma, mental illness, and relational agency. Sarah's creative work is informed by the life and art of Joy Hester (1920–1960). Her writing has been published by Recent Work Press, *TEXT Journal*, *The Victorian Writer* and *Lip Magazine*, among others. Sarah currently works as the Marketing and Communications Coordinator at Writers Victoria and the Jewish Museum of Australia.

Wendy Guest worked as a journalist before her career expanded into politics and communication consulting. She worked for premier Barrie Unsworth in the 80s, prime minister Paul Keating in the 90s and ran her own consultancy before emigrating to Chicago in 2000. Soon after returning to Sydney, NewSouth Books published her first book: *Not Just for This Life: Gough Whitlam Remembered*, in 2016. Wendy holds a Master of Creative Writing from the University of Sydney. She leads workshops in Writing and Yoga, and Embodied Writing in Nature, based on her dissertation *The Yoga of Writing*.

Gillian Hagenus is a writer and editor living and working on Kaurna land. She holds a Master of Philosophy in Creative Writing from the University of Adelaide, specialising in Australian Suburban Gothic fiction. She received the 2022 AAWP / UWAP Chapter One Prize for her unpublished short story collection and is the Editor of *Strangely Enough*, an upcoming anthology of stories published in partnership with the Australian Short Story Festival. When she's not writing or editing manuscripts, she works the front desk of a hotel, collecting stories, ghosts, and a hoard of lost property.

Eileen Herbert-Goodall worked as a Sessional Academic (in creative writing and literature) for many years. She presently works as an Academic Editor as well as an editor of fiction. Eileen has written fiction and non-fiction for a wide range of publications and journals. Her short stories have been recognised in international awards, including the Fish Publishing Short Story Prize, Inktears International Short Story Contest, the Raven Short Story Contest, and Glimmer Train's Short Story Award. She is the author of the novella *The Sherbrooke Brothers* (2017, Moonshine Cove Publishing, USA). Eileen holds a Doctorate of Creative Arts.

Atul Joshi was born in Myanmar of Indian parents and migrated to Australia as a child. Since completing a Master of Arts in Creative Writing at UTS, he has been shortlisted for the *Saturday Paper*'s 2020 Donald Horne and the Newcastle Writers' Festival 2022 Fresh Ink Prizes, had short fiction published in *The Big Issue*, *Westerly*, *Island*, *Seizure* and *Ricepaper Magazine*, non-fiction in the *Portside Review*, *Peril Magazine*, *Sydney Review of Books* and Benjamin Law's *Growing up Queer in Australia*. Atul lives in Robertson, NSW, and is currently undertaking a PhD in creative writing focusing on queer memoir and biography.

Dean Kerrison is a PhD candidate at Griffith University, Gold Coast, working on a travel memoir. His writing often focuses on the (dis)connection of outsiders in foreign environments, and has been featured in *TEXT Journal*, *Meniscus*, *The Bangalore Review*, *Pratik*, *Usawa Literary Review*, *Ace III*, *The In/Completeness Book II*, *Joao Roque Literary Journal*, *The Lit Quarterly* and more.

Katy Knighton's writing background comes from a decade of producing and presenting a weekly programme on community radio.

She won the Peter Cowan 600 (Novice) in 2021. In 2022 she was shortlisted for a Lord Mayor's Creative Writing Award, highly commended for an entry to the AWWP/ASSF Emerging Writer's Prize, and had a story published in *Overland*'s Fiction Friday. In 2023 she was longlisted for the Commonwealth Short Story Prize, longlisted for the Furphy Literary Award and shortlisted for the Wyndham Writing Award. She is delighted to have a story included in the anthology *Strangely Enough*.

Vicki Kyriakakis is a writer, marketing strategist and improviser living in Melbourne Australia. She is an alum of the FutureScapes International Workshop and has had short fiction published in *Peril Magazine* and non-fiction published in *The Guardian Australia*, *SBS Voices* and *The Age*. Her short story 'Kerania Versus the Dream' won first prize in the 2023 Albury City Short Story Award and was shortlisted for the AAWP/UWRF Emerging Writers Prize 2023. In 2018 her middle-grade fantasy was shortlisted for the Hardie Grant Egmont Ampersand Prize. She is also a regular guest on ABC Melbourne's *Spin Doctors* program.

Katherine Mann is a PhD candidate in Creative Writing at Swinburne University. Katherine's writing has been previously published in *Ace III: Arresting Contemporary Stories by Emerging Writers*.

Gabriella Munoz is a writer and editor based in Naarm. Her work has appeared in *Cordite Poetry Review*, *Meanjin*, *Mascara Literary Review*, *Kill Your Darlings*, and other publications. In 2019 she was the recipient of a Wheeler Centre Hot Desk Fellowship. She is the founding Editor of *Puentes Review*.

Julia Prendergast lives in Melbourne, Australia, on unceded Wurundjeri land. Her novel, *The Earth Does Not Get Fat* (2018) was longlisted for the Indie Book Awards (debut fiction). Her short story collection, *Bloodrust and Other Stories*, was published in 2022. Julia is a practice-led researcher—an enthusiastic supporter of transdisciplinary, collaborative research practices, with a particular interest in neuro|psychoanalytic approaches to writing and creativity. Julia is President|Chair of the Australasian Association of Writing Programs (AAWP), the peak academic body representing the discipline of Creative Writing (Australasia). She is Associate Professor and Discipline Leader (Creative Writing and Publishing) at Swinburne University, Melbourne.

Jocelyn Richardson is a writer from Naarm (Melbourne), Australia. She is a winner of the Peter Steele Poetry Award and her writing has been shortlisted for the Peter Carey Short Story Award and the Neilma Sidney Short Story Prize. Her non-fiction and poetry has appeared in *TEXT Journal*, *Kill Your Darlings* and *Ricochet* and her fiction in *Meanjin* and *Epiphany*. She is currently a research candidate in Creative Writing at the University of Melbourne.

Jacob Serena is a long-time writer first-time submitter and author of the short story 'The Last Skywhale'. By day he works as a doctor and loves helping his patients, then by night he trawls through various book genres, video games, movies and D&D games in search of the next great story. Someday, he even hopes to write one. Jacob lives in Brisbane, Australia with his wife Jacki and their elderly furbaby Tekky, and he wouldn't have it any other way.

Alicia Sometimes is an Australian writer and broadcaster. She has performed her spoken word and poetry at many venues, festivals and events around the world. She has been published in *Best Australian Science Writing*, *Best Australian Poems*, *The Age*, *Griffith Review*, *Meanjin*, *Westerly* and more. In 2021 she completed the Boyd Garret residency for the City of Melbourne and a Virtual Writer in Residency for Manchester City of Literature and Manchester Literature Festival. In 2023 she received ANAT's Synapse Artist Residency and co-created a poetic-art installation for Science Gallery Melbourne's exhibition, *Dark Matters*.

Ashley Somwaru is an Indo-Caribbean woman who was born and raised in Queens, New York. As a storyteller and experimental poet, her work is immersed in her mixed tongue, religious upbringings, superstitions, and cultural traditions that have made her into the red hibiscus she is. In 2021, Somwaru published a chapbook with Ghostbird Press titled, *Urgent // Where the Mind Goes // Scattered*. Previous work has been published in *Honey Literary*, *Newtown Literary*, *Solstice*, *SWIMM*, *The Margins*, *VIDA Review* and elsewhere.

Anita Thomas is a Singapore-based author and media producer/ consultant. She experiments with stories till they find their perfect form as books, films, websites, photographs, animation, comics, cartoons, music/song or hybrid variations. She brings this focus to literary festivals and her workshops. As artist-in-residence, she worked with the Middle School students of United World College SEA to take their annual art festival online through short films and a dedicated website showcasing their work in poetry, art, dance, music and theatre. Anita has worked in advertising, film and television, and with corporates and non-profits in advertising, design and public relations: https://www.aathomas.biz/.

Deb Wain holds a PhD in Creative Writing. Her research interests include women, food and culture, which she explores through short stories. Her work, which has been published in *Colloquy, Meniscus, Journal of Post-Colonial Cultures and Societies, Verity La,* and *Tincture,* is often inspired by the Australian communities in which she has lived. Deb is a sessional academic in Creative Writing, a copy-editor and writing coach.

Supatra Walker completed a PhD in English and Creative Writing at the University of Newcastle in 2023 where her creative thesis and memoir *Luk-krueng Between Worlds* examined place, identity and belonging from a bi-racial perspective. She grew up in Thailand and New Zealand before embarking on adventures as a governess, camp cook, bookkeeper, jillaroo and school dental therapist in Australia's far north. Supatra now lives on a unique, 185-acre biodiverse farm on the traditional lands of the Wolgulu people in the Snowy Valleys Region of New South Wales where she spends her days on habitat regeneration projects.

Tika Widya is an Indonesian writer whose imagination knows no bounds. She's a storyteller, using her words to paint vivid pictures on the pages. Tika's stories are meant to be like bridges, connecting the magical and everyday aspects of Indonesia. She takes you on journeys through her homeland's diverse cultures, all while exploring the things that unite us all.

Mary Winning was initially from the Riverland in South Australia but now resides in Perth, Western Australia, with her husband and three teenage children. She works full-time for the Education Department and is studying part-time for a BA in Contemporary Arts at Edith Cowan University. Her parents migrated from Greece to Australia in the 1960s and English is her second language, although you'd never guess. After many years of not writing creatively and shelving the urge, she finally allowed herself full expression and is working on a collection of short stories.